QUINN'S INHERITANCE

Judi Lind

A KISMET™ Romance

METEOR PUBLISHING CORPORATION
Bensalem, Pennsylvania

My deep gratitude for the unflagging encouragement from Marge Campbell, the Tuesday Night Critique Group, my agent, James Allen, Peggy Carpino, and, of course, my beloved husband, Larry.

JUDI LIND

Judi's mother said she was born with her nose in a book. In fact, books, and in particular romance novels, have always played a major role in Judi's life. She even met her husband at a writing class where the evening's lesson was on romance novels. Today, due to her husband's job, the Linds (with their spoiled schnauzer, Ms. Pooka) divide their time between their home in La Mesa, California, a *casita* in Rosarito Beach, Mexico, and their mini-ranch in Snowflake, Arizona.

ONE

Quinn Rosetti tucked a last fiery wisp into the knot on her crown just as the doorbell rang.

"Darn!" The last thing she needed was an interruption. Although she had allowed ample time to drive downtown for her appointment, that margin was somehow evaporating in last-minute preparations. Pulling her suit jacket from the closet, Quinn hurried to the door.

"Oh, Marla," she sighed in relief at the sight of her neighbor and best friend. "Come on in, but I'm in sort of a hurry."

"There's nothing wrong with your dad, is there?"

"No, nothing at all." Quinn's dark eyes sparkled with mischief. "You might say I've been *summoned* into town."

She waited for Marla's inquisitive mind to sort out her statement. Quinn remembered playing 20 Questions as a child—she had a sure winner this time, Marla wouldn't guess if she had all afternoon.

Marla stepped back and assessed her friend with a shrewd, knowing gaze. "You're going on a job interview!" Her voice had an accusatory quality.

It was a standing dialogue between the two women that sooner or later, unless her circumstances changed dramatically, Quinn would have to abandon her little boutique, The Scarecrow Emporium, and get a "real" job. Although Quinn's handmade decorative scarecrows were becoming a "hot" commercial item, she still had to watch every penny.

Thank goodness, she was able to supplement her income by teaching occasional art classes at the Institute. More than once she had felt guilty about holding onto the shop when she could find more lucrative employment, but each time Marla had talked her out of it. A staunch believer in Quinn's eventual success, more than once Marla's encouragement kept Quinn from throwing in the towel.

"No, nothing like that." Quinn patted her loyal admirer on the shoulder.

"Pour yourself a cup of coffee while I polish my shoes and I'll tell you."

Marla followed Quinn into the kitchen and selected a white porcelain mug adorned with pink and red hearts from a wooden rack.

"So, what gives?" Marla asked as she helped herself to coffee.

"It's kind of involved . . ."

"I've got time," she responded with the air of determination that characterized her entire personality. To punctuate her intention, she pulled back a white wicker chair and settled onto the bright rose cushion.

Wiping a speck of dust from her black dress pumps, Quinn leaned across the ceramic counter separating the kitchen from the small dining area. "Remember when I found that injured kitten last spring?"

"Mmm-hmm. The one you hauled to the vet in the middle of a thunderstorm?"

Ignoring her friend's effort to elevate her simple action to heroic standards, Quinn responded, "Well, after the vet stitched his shoulder, I tracked down the owner through his tag and eventually got him safely returned."

"Without so much as a nickel reward, if I remember correctly."

"Reward! For goodness sake, Marla, that's not why I did it. Don't tell me that you could have left that poor, innocent little kitten all wet and bleeding . . ."

"No. But I sure wouldn't have offered to pay the vet out of my own pocket, either."

Quinn blew on the first coat of polish to speed its drying. "I didn't have to. You know perfectly well that Mrs. Featherstone paid the bill. It's just that the veterinarian needed a guarantee of payment before he'd come in on the weekend."

"Well," Marla drained her mug and set it in the sink, "if you ask me . . ."

"Which I didn't," Quinn interrupted hastily, picking up the second shoe.

The only thing Marla ever gave away for free was advice, and plenty of it. And today Quinn simply didn't have time for another rendition of the "folly of do-gooders" —Marla's opinion of anyone who performed a service without compensation.

"Mark my words," Marla went on, blatantly ignoring the interruption, "one of these days you're going to end up in trouble. Generosity is all well and good, but you're not exactly rolling in money yourself." She cocked one carrot-red eyebrow and poked the air between them with a stubby finger. "You let too many people take advantage of you."

Quinn turned away from her friend and automatically began to rinse the empty mugs. There was more than a kernel of truth in Marla's words. If anyone should know the dangers of undiluted giving, it was she. But that was the old Quinn. Her pride was still scorched from the flame of embarrassment when she had pushed to get David Simmons hired at the Institute. Quinn's supposed "fiance." Not that she had needed, or even wanted, the enormous diamond engagement ring he kept promising.

As soon as he had the *right* job, nothing would be too good for Quinn. All he needed was a break, he insisted. So after months of his prodding, she had spoken with the director who, against his better judgment, had agreed to give David a try.

Oh, yes, she had found out the bitter truth of Marla's words that a kind act rarely goes unpunished.

David's right job, turned out to be Quinn's. From the moment he was hired, he started jockeying behind her back for Quinn's full-time position. The persuasive argument he used with the conservative director was that since he and Quinn were getting married anyway, it was only right that, as breadwinner, he should have the permanent position. Her superiors were convinced Quinn knew and approved of the proposed change.

She found out about it when the switch was announced by the governing board and she lost her full-time job.

She lost David a short while later.

Oh, well, she thought, as she automatically dried and rehung the mugs on a latticework wall rack, it forced her to do something she'd been wanting to do for years anyway—open up her own business.

Suddenly, she became aware that Marla was speaking.

"Yoo-hoo, earth to Quinn. Where are you?"

"Sorry. Did you say something?"

Marla's bright blue eyes narrowed suspiciously. "I said, what does the kitten have to do with your being dressed like you're about to address the bar association?"

A third-year law student, Marla's conversation was frequently peppered with legalese.

"As a matter-of-fact, I am going to see an attorney."

"Don't tell me that the old lady's suing you for something?"

Quinn laughed. She enjoyed the way her friend's mental processes swept ahead by leaps and bounds—only occasionally skimming the surface of reality.

"No, nothing like that." She rummaged in her purse and pulled out a crumpled white envelope from Kresge, McGuire & Shaw, Attorneys at Law, and tossed it to her friend. "Ever hear of this firm?"

Marla glanced at the engraved envelope and blew a long, low whistle. "Only the best. So what's up? C'mon, buddy, you've been holding out on me. What's going on?"

Quinn's brown-velvet eyes twinkled with merriment. Marla hadn't let her down. Her curiosity was full to the point that her round face was flushed with excitement. With a barely suppressed grin, Quinn drew out her response, "Well . . . it seems that Mrs. Featherstone, she was in her eighties, you know . . ."

"C'mon, c'mon," Marla's sturdy hands reached forward, beckoning, as if to help pull the words from Quinn's mouth.

Feeling slightly ashamed of teasing her friend, Quinn relented. "It seems she recently passed away and . . ."

". . . and she was a multi-millionaire recluse and she left her fortune to you," Marla finished in a rush.

Quinn hoped Marla intended to go into entertainment law. Her imagination and flair for the dramatic would fit right in.

Testing her shoes and finding the polish dry, Quinn slipped them on. Shaking her head at Marla's suggestion, she continued, "If Mrs. Featherstone was a multi-millionaire, she probably left it all to the cat. No, the lawyer's letter mentioned a small bequest."

"It's about time someone thanked you for being a good Samaritan. More often, these strays you help bite the hand that feeds them. Literally. Remember the bum who ripped you off?"

Quinn's eyes darkened at the reminder. The old Quinn might have offered a hot meal to a transient in exchange for washing her windows, and have her laundry money mysteriously disappear while he was in the house, but the new Quinn would have no such problem. Besides, it had only been five dollars and he must have needed it very badly.

Giving the counter one last swipe, she neatly folded the

dish towel across the rack and turned back to Marla. "I don't mean to be rude, but I really better get going. You know how I hate downtown traffic, and I'm not even sure where the law office is."

"No problem."

As they walked through the warm cabin, Marla gave her explicit, if intricate, directions. At the doorway, they stopped while Quinn slipped on her copper suit jacket, and retrieved her keys from a rack in the entryway. Marla poked her lightly in the ribs, a wicked smile brightening her freckled face.

"Aren't you in the least bit excited? How much do you think she left you?"

Quinn placed a slender hand on Marla's stout shoulder and propelled her out the door. "I haven't a clue. Probably just a small gratuity. She wasn't wealthy, you know. That's why I offered to pay the veterinary bill. She was just a sweet little old lady who lived in a sweet little old frame house with her cats. And you ought to be ashamed of yourself for thinking about her money."

She felt a small stab of guilt herself. Marla's silly talk was contagious and Quinn had found herself mentally budgeting her new-found wealth. But, she salved her conscience, it was only natural. It *might* be enough to pay for a private nurse so she could bring her father home for a visit.

Crisp fall air teased them with the scent of pine and cedar as they stepped out into the early morning. There were a lot of disadvantages to living in the small mountain community, but in the autumn, Idyllwild was a visual and aromatic wonderland and she reveled in the quiet country atmosphere.

Marla, however, seemed immune to the lure of nature's bounty. Like a stubborn little terrier, she had latched onto the problem and wasn't about to let go. "Of course, she had money. Poor people don't have fancy law firms handling their estates."

To punctuate her theory, she gave Quinn a knowing wink.

"Mmmm." Quinn had to admit that Marla's logic had a ring of truth. But it was too much of a fairy tale to believe that a comparative stranger would leave her anything of significant value. Although Mrs. Featherstone *had* seemed glad of her company on the day the kitten was returned, and when she had phoned to check on its progress, the old woman had chatted for nearly an hour. Evidently, she hadn't any close family ties—except for a great-nephew she had mentioned.

But still, the entire idea of Mrs. Featherstone being wealthy was . . . ridiculous.

They crunched down the gravel driveway and stopped by Quinn's bright yellow VW bug.

"Well," Marla said, "I'd better get back to the books. But I still think you're wrong." She lifted a brow and shook her finger in admonishment. "I'll bet the old lady left you a bundle. You should take a vacation—go to Tahiti. Do something wild and wonderful with the money. Lighten up and have some fun."

Quinn frowned at the harshness of her friend's words. She wished there was something she could do to lessen Marla's harshness; she sounded so, so greedy . . . there she went again! Quinn, the mother-confessor and solver of problems. When was she going to learn? Instead of trying to change Marla, Quinn should be under her friend's tutelage—taking lessons in reality. Besides, although Marla was sometimes abrasive, Quinn knew that a gentle spirit was hiding beneath the hard veneer.

Suddenly overwhelmed by affection, Quinn hugged the rumpled figure dressed in a plaid shirt and baggy Levis.

With a grin, Marla loped across the road. She stopped at the beginning of her own steep driveway and yelled back, "If you hit the jackpot, you have to buy the wine. And none of that $1.89-a-gallon stuff, either."

Quinn smiled as she unlocked the car door and slid

across the vinyl seat. Hit the jackpot, indeed. It would be great if she got enough for a new battery for her trusty little VW. She shifted into gear and eased onto the highway. The way her luck had been lately, she'd probably find out that she'd inherited the cat!

A young blonde receptionist looked up from her twinkling switchboard. "May I help you?"

"Yes. Quinn Rosetti to see Mr. Shaw, please."

The girl consulted a clipboard on her U-shaped desk and ticked off Quinn's name with a red pencil. "Have a seat," she pointed to a mahogany paneled waiting area, "Mr. Shaw will be with you shortly."

With a flourish of her brilliantly painted nails, the young woman plugged another cord into her flashing board and responded with a sing-song lilt, "Good morning. Kresge, McGuire & Shaw—aw." Her ponytail bounced in time with her words.

Quinn waded across the deep pile carpet and sank gratefully into a high-backed wing chair and grimaced in pain. Unaccustomed to high heels, she yearned to take off her shoes and massage her crumpled toes.

She glanced around. The room was unoccupied with the exception of the receptionist and she was focused on her switchboard, pressing buttons and scribbling messages on scraps of paper. Quinn rubbed her ankle. It didn't help, it was the ball of her foot that was aching. If she could just uncramp that little toe. . . .

In an effort to distract herself from the discomfort, she moved to pick up a magazine from the brass trunk serving as a coffee table. A sharp pain shot through the bottom of her arch. No wonder her foot was hurting—there was something in her shoe. If she could just take it off long enough to shake out whatever was in there . . . Quinn sank back into the velvet wing chair, and surreptitiously surveyed the room.

The wagging blonde ponytail told her that the receptionist was engaged in conversation and was unlikely to take notice. It would only take a moment. Deciding no possible harm could come from the action, she bent over and slid the right pump from her slender ankle.

Oh, did that feel good, she reveled in the freedom from the confining footwear. Holding the shoe up to eye level, Quinn looked for the object that had been causing her such grief. A frown creased her clear brow; there didn't seem to be anything in there. She ran long fingers down into the toes.

Nothing.

But it couldn't have been her imagination. Pursing her lips in concentration, she raised the shoe up to the light. She still couldn't see anything. Finally Quinn decided to give it a shake.

Nothing was dislodged.

She shook with a little more vigor.

There was a movement in the toe but nothing fell out. Hmmm, just about got it, she thought, giving the pump a firm slap with the heel of her hand.

Like a dark bullet exploding in the quiet room, the shoe shot from her hand, flew across the carpeted area, and skittered to a stop on the oak parquet floor in front of the elevators.

Embarrassment giving her cheeks the same coppery hue as her hair, Quinn looked up to see the receptionist's wide-eyed stare. Obviously, not everyone pitched their shoes across the lobby of Kresge, McGuire & Shaw. Arching her brows, Quinn tried to maintain a pose of unconcerned sophistication, as if it were a socially-accepted practice to sail one's footwear across public waiting rooms. The ploy evidently worked because the young woman quickly turned her attention back to her telephone duties.

Now, if she could only retrieve her errant pump before anyone else entered the lobby. Closing her eyes in silent prayer, Quinn crossed the room with the ungainly cadence of an expectant duck. As she neared the polished wood floor, she began to think she would make it.

Then, she heard the whine of the elevator.

Her stomach weaved and bobbed like a punchy prize-fighter. It had to be coming here—this was the last floor. Rushing across the last few feet her unshod foot slipped on the highly waxed surface.

With a last sliver of thought that this had to be a bad dream and she could wake up any time now, Quinn felt her right leg fly out from under and she tumbled in an unceremonious heap onto her backside.

The elevator announced its arrival with a ding.

More embarrassed than hurt, she covered her eyes with a trembling hand and tried to melt into the woodwork. She remembered that as a child she had believed if she hid her eyes, no one could see her either. She cringed at the childhood memory and wondered if this was the infamous life passing in front of your eyes, she had often heard about.

How could this have happened to her? Quinn Rosetti was a quiet, conservative woman who was always in control of herself and her surroundings. This ludicrous situation had to be a bad dream. But just to cover all bets, she discreetly tucked her skirt over her knees as the eleva-tor door whirred open.

She sensed the presence of someone between her and the stainless-steel elevator door. Then, a deeply-timbred voice penetrated her confused mind.

"Are you all right? May I help you?"

Quinn shook her head, eyes still tightly squenched shut. "No, please. Just go away."

But the fates weren't going to be that kind today. Nor was she going to be allowed to evaporate into space, she decided, as she sensed no movement from the unseen man. Facing the inevitable, Quinn opened her eyes and peeked between the spaces of her long, artistic fingers.

A pair of rich brown cordovans were inches from her

knees. She supposed those feet were attached to a body of some sort. Why couldn't she just die now?

As if suddenly imbued with a will of their own, her eyes traveled upward. The feet were attached to a pair of slacks of nubby beige silk. The legs inside the slacks were long, incredibly long it seemed from Quinn's perspective. Her eyes continued their journey upward, taking in the muscular thrust of thighs and narrow hips.

Tanned fists, shadowed by dark flecks of hair, poised on those narrow hips and pushed aside a matching silk jacket. A tailored ivory shirt lay flat against a firm abdomen and wide chest.

Quinn swallowed hard. There was no doubt in her mind—the man was going to be gorgeous. A blond Viking with icy-blue eyes, staring down at her with cold contempt. Why couldn't she have made a fool of herself in front of another klutz?

Always one who would put off bad news as long as possible, Quinn nevertheless knew she couldn't sit on the floor forever. At least not without drawing a crowd. She sucked in a deep breath, and held it to the count of three. Then, summoning all of her courage—she looked up into the face of the man looming over her like an eagle watching its prey.

She had only been half right. He wasn't a blue-eyed, blond Viking; but he was gorgeous. Dark. Thick hair one shade darker than midnight. Deeply tanned skin, the perfect shade to accentuate his beige clothing. But his most arresting feature was his eyes. Light. Lighter than his skin. Like café au lait—heavy on the cream. And those pale eyes were fastened with intensity on Quinn. Unlike her premonition, his gaze wasn't cold and contemptuous. His eyes were warm and sparkled with . . . amusement?

Nice mouth. But it was quivering. So was his firmly-planed chin. He was going to laugh! Too late, Quinn realized she was still peeking up through her spread fingers. Dropping her hand to her side, she scowled in despair. Surely the most humiliating experience of her life would be to have this man laugh at her.

As if reading her mind, his lips firmed and his features hardened into a mask of solemnity. Unfurling a fist, he extended his hand toward her.

"May I help you up," he asked without a trace of humor in his voice, "or are you staging a sit-in?"

"Yes, as a matter of fact, I'm demonstrating against the lack of jobs for out-of-work comedians," she snapped, unaccountably annoyed at his insensitivity toward her embarrassment. "I'm sure, since you fit in that category, that you'd be willing to join the picket line."

He nudged his hand toward her, a broad grin creasing his face. "Maybe, but I think you'd be more effective if you moved your campaign to a more public location. Can't expect too much attention for your cause on the twelfth floor of the American Bank Building."

Ignoring his outstretched hand, Quinn braced herself with her flattened palms on the parquet tile and rose to her feet. He certainly took long enough to offer assistance. And then, he had the temerity to find her predicament funny. He might *look* wonderful, but in her opinion, the man didn't have a shred of gallantry. He hadn't even bothered to ask if she was injured.

"Thanks for the advice," she nodded curtly, "I'm sure you have lots of experience fighting for lost causes."

With a regal toss of her mussed russet curls, she turned on her heel and started for the sanctuary of the waiting room. After two steps, however, she became painfully aware of the difficulty of a dignified exit when one was forced to walk with a lopsided gait. After all of this, she had still failed to retrieve her shoe.

"Hey, Cinderella," that maddening man was calling, "do you think this slipper will fit your dainty foot?"

She turned and snatched the shoe from his hand. "Thank you," she muttered.

"Now, Cinderella, if you're not nicer to the handsome prince, he's not going to share his kingdom with you."

Her embarrassment had heated to humiliation and now boiled into white anger. Eyes flashing almost black in her fury, she shook her shoe at him. "I . . . I . . . wouldn't share your . . ."

His golden eyes sparkled as he arched a charcoal brow and mockingly gave her his undivided attention. "You wouldn't share my what?"

She was saved from responding by the bob of a ponytail.

"Miss Rosetti, Miss Rosetti," the receptionist was waving her arm, "Mr. Shaw can see you now."

"Thank you," Quinn nodded to the girl with as much dignity as she could muster. She slipped her pump back on her foot, and completely ignoring Prince Charming, crossed the room to gather her handbag from beside the wing chair.

"Right this way, Miss Rosetti." The receptionist had opened a door to a long hallway and stood waiting.

Prince Not-So-Charming leaned casually against the U-shaped desk, and, of course, she would have to cross directly in front of him to reach the doorway.

Quinn studiously avoided looking at him as she passed the desk. But he wasn't going to let her pass without a final quip. "See you at the ball, if your wicked stepmother lets you go."

Grasping the door frame with clenched fingers, she turned and said sweetly, "Since I won't be able to get there before midnight, I'm sure you'll have turned back into a frog."

She swept through the door and followed the receptionist down the narrow hallway, but not before she heard his muffled reply.

"Hey, Cinderella, you're not playing fair. You're mixing fairy tales."

A gale of deep, hearty laughter followed her down the tunnel-like passage.

Shoving all of her pent-up Irish-Italian temper down deep inside, she straightened her shoulders and continued walking. The bruise on her heel was smarting, but she forced herself to keep moving with a steady, dignified pace.

Pausing at the doorway to Attorney Shaw's office, she turned and looked behind her.

Her tormenter was leaning against the wall, watching her. Even from the twenty-yard distance, she could see the white flash of teeth against his tan. He was still laughing.

"Troll," she muttered.

TWO

"Ah! Miss Rosetti, come in," George Shaw's resonant voice ushered Quinn into the stage-set office. Built-in bookcases lined the walls; each filled with exquisitely bound volumes. There were so many books, Quinn felt all of the world's legal knowledge must surely be contained within these four walls.

A brass scale of justice held George Shaw's business cards, providing the perfect counterpoint for the polished mahogany surface of his barren desk top, giving the impression that the room had been designed by a theatrical designer.

The lawyer himself might have stepped off of a sound stage. Tall, thin, and strategically gray at the temples, he reminded her very much of a popular actor of years past. She couldn't remember his name, but she was sure that Shaw had used him as a pattern for the perfect attorney.

"Please, have a seat. May I offer you coffee?"

"No, thank you." Settling on a burgundy leather wing chair, she self-consciously patted her hair and wondered why she felt so ill at ease.

There was a discreet buzz on the intercom and the attorney murmured an apology as he picked up the telephone receiver. "Ah, Malcolm!" his refined timbre shivered through the room in the tradition of barristers as portrayed by actors a generation past.

While he was occupied with his conversation, Quinn took advantage of the opportunity to have a serious talk with herself.

The dignified atmosphere had a calming effect on her rattled nerves and the incident in the lobby began to pale in importance. How could anyone feel anything but contentment in this room, she wondered, gazing at the palmetto plants and ficus trees providing greenery from the corners. The dashes of color lent a softness to the texture of the room and Quinn was able to regain her equilibrium in the understated elegance of her surroundings.

In a flash of sudden clarity, she understood her discomfort. It was that man in the lobby. His composure in the midst of her fiasco had only emphasized her temper fit, and her ego had suffered by the comparison. Now that the remembrance of her discomfiting experience had faded, she realized she had been unfair in her treatment of him. He had really done nothing offensive and, in fact, had probably been employing humor to try and ease her embarrassment. She had lashed out at him because he was handy.

She salved her conscious by promising to apologize if their paths ever crossed again.

Mr. Shaw's telephone oration seemed to be winding down and she settled back into the chair to await its conclusion.

"Certainly, Malcolm, anytime. See you on the links Saturday." Replacing the receiver, he swiveled in his oversized padded chair and beamed at Quinn.

"So, Miss Rosetti, you must be a special young woman. Elvira Featherstone certainly spoke highly of you."

"She did?" Quinn couldn't imagine how empty the woman's life must have been if her small gesture had had such an impact.

"Yes. Very impressed by your kindness. Very." He steepled his manicured fingers and leaned back, evidently preparing to be sage and contemplative.

Raymond Massey, that was it, she decided. If he traded his elegant silk tie for a bow tie, he could step onto stage as Massey's double.

She was so involved in her observation that it took a moment for Shaw's words to penetrate. "What did you say?"

"I said," he patted his fingertips together, seemingly piqued at her lack of attention, "Mrs. Featherstone made provisions in a codicil to her will whereby she would cover private nursing expenses for your father for a five-year period so he could live at home. That, of course, would afford you the opportunity to devote all of your time and energy to your shop. Mrs. Featherstone apparently felt that five years was sufficient for you to make a success of your business."

He paused and eyed her seriously, as though ready to pronounce judgment. "*If* you possess the necessary talent and commitment to begin with."

Quinn's pulse pounded in her ears. She felt as if she had won the lottery. To be able to bring Daniel back to his beloved cabin. She had always felt if her father were surrounded by his warm and cherished reminders of her mother, much of his mental fog would be alleviated. Even the doctors were puzzled by his rapidly diminishing mental faculties.

Yes, to bring her father home was the one dream she had long cherished without hope of fulfillment. She had only a vague recollection of telling Mrs. Featherstone about her dream. And the woman had remembered that chance conversation with a stranger! This couldn't be happening.

"Provided, of course," Shaw tapped his forefingers together, "that you meet one simple criteria."

An Arctic airstream entered and flowed through her

veins. Of course, here was the catch. "What . . . what criteria?"

"Actually, it's more of a deed than a standard."

She wished he would leave his courtroom demeanor and speak plainly. What kind of deed? She shook her head, confused.

"Mrs. Featherstone has asked that you perform one simple favor for her because she trusted your judgment."

Quinn was more befuddled than ever. She waited for him to continue. Evidently, he had rehearsed this scene and was going to play it to its dramatic conclusion.

When it became apparent that she wasn't going to throw audience-participation questions in his direction, Shaw leaned across the desk and stared intently into her eyes.

Finally, as if reaching a decision, he continued, "Although Elvira chose to live simply, she had a great deal of money under her control. She and her husband had lived abroad for most of their marriage so she lost touch with her family. After his death—they had no children of their own—she was very lonely and decided to come back here and look up any remaining relatives. To put it simply, the few remaining Hunters—that was Elvira's maiden name— were a grave disappointment to her. Except one."

"But I don't understand. What has all of this to do with me?"

"In good time, my dear, in good time."

Shaw leaned back in his swivel chair and contemplated the ceiling. He clasped his hands across his stomach, his fingertips tapping each other in a rhythmic pattern. "There *was*," he continued, "one great-nephew that she was drawn to."

Quinn nodded. "Gabriel Hunter?"

Shaw raised a sparse gray eyebrow. "You know him?"

"No. But Mrs. Featherstone talked about him quite frequently." Quinn didn't mention that the older woman had made a point of mentioning her *eligible* great-nephew at least once during every conversation. In fact, Quinn had fended off several blatant matchmaking attempts engineered by Elvira Featherstone.

"I see." The attorney moved an engraved desk set a quarter of an inch. Apparently satisfied that it was now perfectly aligned, he looked back at the lovely young woman seated before him. "Unfortunately," he continued, "Mr. Hunter's business kept him in the Del Mar area and Elvira didn't get to know him as well as she would have liked. And after the others, well, frankly, she wasn't sure whether she shouldn't just leave her estate to the Friends of Cats, or something. Which is where you come in."

Oh, dear lord, she wasn't going to have to open an animal sanctuary or something was she?

"Elvira's idea," Shaw went on, "was to fabricate a situation wherein you could become acquainted with her great-nephew and give us your recommendation as to whether he is worthy to receive the bulk of her estate."

Quinn felt her dreams fading like the muted colors of the books lining the walls around her. She had no illusions about the situation. The older woman had been so gratified by her small act that she had placed undue trust in Quinn's abilities. But as much as she wanted to bring her father back to his mountain home, she couldn't allow herself to become judge and jury for Elvira's long-lost relative. Impossible.

Choking on the ashes of her lost hope, she turned to the attorney. "I can't tell you how much I appreciate the offer . . . but . . . but I certainly have no qualifications to do that. I just couldn't take that kind of responsibility . . . No, I'm sorry, but I'll have to decline."

Quinn stood and picked up her handbag.

"Not so fast, my dear. Wait until you hear it all."

"Look, I'm sorry, but I simply cannot pass judgment on another human being. I'm sure Mrs. Featherstone had an alternate option, so . . . I'm sorry, but no."

"Miss Rosetti, by your refusal you'll be doing that very thing."

"What?"

"Invoking the second option. Her will provides that if you refuse the assignment, the money will be automatically forfeited by Mr. Hunter."

"But . . . but that's not fair," she sputtered.

"Fair or not, that's the way it is. So, you see, if you refuse this simple request, he will lose all rights to any of the estate."

Sensing a weakness in his prey, Shaw attacked like a lion. "Besides, surely you don't doubt your own ability to make a fair, unbiased report of your opinions, do you? If you were called to jury duty, wouldn't you be able to perform?"

Quinn sat back in her chair. Of course, she could be objective enough to sit on a jury. But this was different somehow. She shook her head. This whole scheme was absurd. It had to be illegal. Well, maybe not. Her brief acquaintance with George Shaw convinced her he would never take part in something illegal. And, after all, it was Mrs. Featherstone's money to do with as she pleased. . . .

"All right, Mr. Shaw. Exactly how was this recommendation to be made?"

"Excellent, excellent." He treated her to a beaming smile. A smug, so-glad-you-finally-listened-to-me smile. "I'm sure you won't regret your decision."

"I already do," she said, then listened intently as Mr. Shaw outlined the plan.

Thirty minutes later, Quinn felt as if she had been abandoned in a Chinese maze. It was hard to believe that fluffy little old lady had been capable of such machinations.

Mrs. Featherstone had believed that a person's character was crystallized in their treatment of animals—hence, her instinctive trust in Quinn. Therefore, she had devised a plan that would give Quinn and the great-nephew split custody, so to speak, of the cat for two months. In that time, Quinn would have ample time to observe and formulate an opinion of Gabriel Hunter.

At the end of the sixty-day period, Quinn would make a written evaluation of the man and pass it on to the law firm. Mr. Shaw had been careful to explain that other information was going to be gathered, and that Mrs. Featherstone had left a clear method to interpret her great-nephew's suitability, so the outcome would only partially be the result of Quinn's appraisal. That helped assuage her worry and she was able to reassess the situation.

In reality, she decided, all she had to do was take turns baby-sitting McLeish (the cat who got her into this mess) and keep an objective eye on Gabriel Hunter for two months.

It really didn't sound so awful, now that she thought about it. And the five years of care for her father would be guaranteed, regardless of her final evaluation. She had to admit that the old lady was smart. Had she offered money, Quinn would have been able to turn it down. But Elvira had a firm grip on her Achille's heel.

The lawyer interrupted her deliberations. "So, am I to gather you concede to Elvira's request?"

Quinn hesitated, still afraid of what she could be letting herself in for. But, she reminded herself, a refusal would take a great deal of money away from a person she had never even met. Oh, yes, Elvira Featherstone had contrived a very clever trap.

"I suppose so," she said at last.

"Excellent, excellent. I've taken the liberty to ask Mr. Hunter to come into the office so you could meet and make arrangements for McLeish. But I do have to point out one small proviso, however."

Oh, no, Quinn groaned. Had Elvira put yet another twist in this puzzle?

"I feel like that man on the old television show who used to give away millions." He chuckled self-consciously, then continued, "Remember him? Probably not, you're far too young."

She put her hand over her mouth so he wouldn't see her grin. It was the first time she had seen him laugh. He was *enjoying* this. She wouldn't be in the least surprised to find he'd had a hand in devising this plot.

"No, I remember. I saw reruns or something. What about it?"

"Well, I must caution you about one thing," he laughed again, "you must not disclose this arrangement to anyone—I repeat—anyone."

Quinn's brow furrowed. "You mean, this Mr. Hunter doesn't know what's going on?"

"Oh, no!" Shaw exclaimed, "Especially him. You mustn't let him suspect a thing. After all, he might try to influence your recommendation. Dear me, that wouldn't do at all."

Raymond Massey clucked several times in dismay.

This wasn't a Chinese maze, she decided; she had fallen down the rabbit hole. Curiouser and curiouser. And what was worse, it was beginning to sound logical!

"But I don't understand. He has to be told something. I mean, how can we explain . . ." her voice trailed off in confusion.

The attorney broke in smoothly. "Of course, we'll offer him an explanation, my dear. He's been told a portion of the truth. He only knows that the two of you have been given—shall we say, joint custody—of McLeish. Further, we've alluded to the fact that there is to be a further reading of Elvira's intentions in a couple of months and that his inheritance could be adjusted based on his, uh, suitability as a custodial parent for McLeish. However, he has no idea that you are in any way involved, except as another beneficiary."

Quinn thought she must be slipping. This scheme was starting to sound workable.

"All right, Mr. Shaw, I'll do my best. But I've got a bad feeling about this. A very bad feeling."

"Nonsense," the attorney responded briskly, back to business now that the dramatic climax had been revealed. He pushed a button on his intercom and leaned forward to speak into the microphone.

"Miss Esterhaus, please show Mr. Hunter in to my office."

He released the button and turned back to Quinn. "It's very simple. Just remember to be fair and objective, stay in as close contact with Mr. Hunter as you can, and don't tell anyone what's going on. Simple."

"The only thing simple about this is me, for getting talked into this wacky scheme," she retorted. She couldn't shake the feeling that this wasn't going to be as straightforward as Shaw believed.

There was a soft tap on the door. A ponytail bounced around the door frame. "Mr. Hunter is here."

The door opened wide and Quinn's premonition of impending disaster grew to a certainty. Stepping in the doorway with casual assuredness was none other than him. The troll from the lobby.

THREE

She would have rather dealt with the Mad Hatter.

The tawny-eyed Gabriel Hunter apparently didn't share Quinn's misapprehensions about their joint venture. With a good-natured grin, he allowed the attorney to make the introductions. Only the merriment in his eyes betrayed the inauspiciousness of their first encounter.

Holding her hand a moment longer than necessary, he acknowledged their acquaintance. "Miss Rosetti and I met briefly in the lobby, George."

He lowered his large frame into an identical wing chair adjoining Quinn's and listened attentively as George Shaw outlined the skeleton of Elvira's plan. Gabriel Hunter's gaze flickered around the room and with each pass, encompassed Quinn in its orbit.

She wished he would pay attention to the lawyer. This wasn't a social meeting, after all. She felt the heat of his eyes blistering through the thinness of her silk blouse. Her hand automatically checked her buttons. Finding them properly fastened, she decided he was simply a lech and if she ignored him he would soon become bored with his childish appraisal.

Folding her hands primly in her lap, Quinn stared intently at the attorney, as if fascinated with his every word. She declared success when she noticed that Gabriel Hunter had not looked in her direction for several moments. Was that a flash of disappointment that he had so easily tired of looking at her? No, she firmly asserted, it was relief. Definitely relief. To confirm her decision, she turned her attention back to the attorney.

Mr. Shaw finished his summation and both he and Quinn looked to Gabriel for his reaction, which was quickly expressed.

"I wish I had known her better," he exclaimed when Shaw had finished, "she must have been a great old dame."

Quinn cringed at his choice of words, but was surprised to see the lawyer beaming his approval.

"Indeed, she was," Shaw agreed. "In fact, she often said that she wanted to be remembered as an 'old broad who learned to hula-hoop at eighty.' "

Gabriel laughed, a rich hearty expression of appreciation. "Did you know that she had three of the darn things? Attributed her good health to them."

"Three hula-hoops?" Quinn asked. Somehow this didn't fit her impression of a sweet old lady who baked cookies and kept cats.

"Yeah," his pale eyes crinkled at the memory. "She even had one that glowed in the dark. Used to play rock music and use them for exercise. Said that was how she kept her girlish figure."

Quinn felt a fleeting sadness that she hadn't pursued a closer friendship with the older woman. She loved people who sought the joy in life and Elvira Featherstone apparently had been one of those spirited people.

She looked at Gabriel Hunter with new interest, wondering if he had inherited his great-aunt's zest. If his ready laugh and twinkling eyes were any indication—he had.

George Shaw stood and placed his palms flat on his desk in a gesture of dismissal. "Well, now all we need is

McLeish. I'll leave you two to work out the details of his care. Let's see . . ." he slid back the sleeve of his herring-bone jacket and consulted a thin gold wristwatch. "I can have McLeish delivered here . . . say, in an hour?"

"Fine," Gabriel stated without hesitation.

"I suppose." Quinn was still unsure about the wisdom of this venture, but had committed herself and would give it her best shot. But somehow the thought of spending two months in close company with Gabriel Hunter was unsettling. Mr. Shaw extended his hand. "Okay, just drop back by in about an hour and pick up your charge. I have to be in court, but Miss Esterhaus will have McLeish."

He shook their hands in turn, then walked them to the doorway. "Keep in touch, if I can be of any assistance . . ."

Back in his Raymond Massey role, he nodded curtly and went back into his office.

Alone in the hallway, they didn't seem to know what to say to each other. The silence built for a few seconds, and was abruptly broken by both of them speaking at the same time.

"Look, I want to apolog . . ."

"Hey, I didn't mean to sound like . . . I'm sorry, what did you say?"

"No," Quinn shook her head, "go ahead."

"No, that's okay. Ladies first."

Quinn felt her irritation returning. "I'm perfectly capable of waiting my turn . . ."

"No, I insist."

"All right!" she exploded, "I'll go first . . ."

"No, that's okay," Gabriel interrupted, "I shouldn't have insisted."

"I *said* I'll go first," she muttered between clenched teeth.

She looked up, glaring into his tiger eyes—which were shining back down at her, gleaming with amusement. He had only been teasing, she realized with a start. Deciding to ignore his strange sense of humor, she tried again.

"I wanted to apologize for being so rude earlier. I'm not usually like that, but . . ."

"You weren't so rude," he cut in. "I thought you were spunky."

"Spunky?" Quinn repeated, spitting the word out as if it had been coated with cod liver oil. Children were spunky, and puppies were spunky, but *she* wasn't spunky.

"Sure," he responded, oblivious to the snarl in her voice, "not everyone could land on her keister and then joke about it. I admire a person who can keep their sense of humor when they'd rather be burrowing a tunnel and crawling away."

"It wasn't that bad," she protested.

"No, you're probably right," he said as he took her elbow and led the way down the hall. "World War III—now that would be bad. You drink coffee?"

Quinn tried to look up to see if he was serious, but he was walking so fast that she had to concentrate to keep up without tripping. This was the longest hallway. At five-six, her legs were longer than the average woman's, but he was testing her endurance. Then he opened a door and, like Mecca, the lobby appeared.

Gabriel stopped and looked down at her flushed face. "You didn't answer. Don't you like coffee?"

She brushed a wisp of hair from her face. "I could use a cup right now, having just finished the hundred-yard dash."

"Huh?" He looked behind them, his black brows dipped in confusion. "Oh, you mean I walk too fast. I'm sorry—bad habit. Never seems to be enough time and I'm always in a hurry. But we have an hour. Can I buy you something to drink?"

This man was definitely unsettling. Like a teletype, he darted from one subject to another, clipping his sentences and speaking in some kind of shorthand. He needed to slow down, she thought. After the tranquility of her life in Idyllwild, his city pace made her nervous.

Nevertheless, feeling that it was the least she could do

to make up for her earlier lack of courtesy, Quinn agreed to his request.

They rode the elevator to the lobby and stepped outside into the midday warmth. It was a balmy, travel-poster day, showing San Diego in all of its finery.

"Want to try Horton Plaza?" Gabriel asked as they waited for a traffic light to change.

"Sure." She glanced up at his strong profile, silhouetted by the golden sunlight and realized with a start that she was looking forward to that shared cup of coffee. Gabriel Hunter was, after all, a vital, exciting—if somewhat overwhelming—man and she had deprived herself of masculine company for a very long while.

They walked the three blocks in silence, soaking up the sea breeze blowing gently from the bay. Once, while sneaking a peek at his chiseled jaw, softened by his generous mouth, Quinn was startled to find him watching her with an intensity that was disconcerting. Ignoring the sudden thudding of her heart, she pulled her gaze from his. Then, suddenly, they were greeted with a barrage of color as they entered the five-leveled shopping mall.

"I think there's a coffee shop kind of thing up there," Gabriel pointed to a higher level.

They walked past a small crowd of people who were clapping and swaying in time with a Dixieland jazz band performing in one of the open areas. A little further away, a juggler tossed balls into the air as he wobbled precariously on a unicycle.

"Isn't this place great?" Quinn enthused as he led them into a small but crowded restaurant.

"Sure is. We did some of the work on this project," he said as they looked around for an empty table.

"What is your line of work, Mr. Hunter?"

"Marketing consultant. Mostly try to save struggling businesses. But once in a while somebody's smart enough to do some research *before* they spend their money. Like here."

He broke off as a young couple in shorts and sunburns rose from two stools and made their way to the door.

"Counter okay?" He nodded toward the vacant seats.

"Yes, that's fine," she answered as they edged through the close seating and sank onto the padded stools.

He ordered two coffees and they sat quietly for a moment, enjoying the air conditioning.

"How's the foot?" he asked.

Quinn had forgotten about the bruise that had led to their dramatic introduction. Her face flamed at the embarrassing recollection.

"Mmm. Fine." Well, it wasn't exactly fine, but darned if she was going to take her shoe off again before she was tucked safely in her own home.

"Hungry?"

She hadn't thought about it, but his question brought an ominous rumble from her stomach. "It's a little early for lunch . . . but . . ."

She stopped as she looked up into a glassed-in refrigerated case. The stainless-steel shelves were lined with pies and pastries, their whipped creamed toppings high and fluffy. Although she rarely allowed herself the indulgence, Quinn had a sweet tooth and that single slice of banana cream pie remaining in a pie tin was tempting.

Gabriel's followed her gaze. "What looks good?"

Quinn's mouth watered. "That last piece of banana cream pie," she said longingly.

"You're kidding?"

He sounded so shocked that she looked at him in surprise.

"Do you mean to tell me you would eat that stuff? I mean, all that sugar. Do you know what that junk does to your teeth?"

Put that way, it was starting to lose its appeal. But his self-righteous manner was irritating and she refused to be bullied.

"I like banana cream pie—sugar and all."

"And calories," he continued as if she hadn't spoken,

"all those empty, worthless calories. Do you realize that one little piece probably has an entire day's caloric allowance? And all that fat, clogging your arteries . . . but you go ahead, it's your body."

She was suddenly acutely aware of the three pounds that had recently snuck onto her hips while she wasn't looking. She had been threatening to work on losing that weight for the last couple of weeks. If she ate that pie now . . . but, still . . . what a killjoy, she thought, not relishing spending the next two months with a health nut.

"Well, maybe you're right," she agreed, as the waitress returned to take their order.

"What'll you have, honey?" the waitress asked, pencil poised over her green pad.

Reluctantly, Quinn pulled her eyes from the pastries and turned her attention to the adjoining display. "I guess I'll have that cottage cheese and pineapple salad," she said, her mournful voice sounding like she had just finished fifth in a four-man race.

"And you, sir?" The waitress turned to Gabriel.

"Oh, I'll have the banana cream pie," he promptly replied, his handsome face expressionless.

Quinn's mouth dropped open. The creep! Finally, she found her voice. "Of all the absolutely selfish, conniving, ruthless, and self-serving tricks I have ever seen . . ."

She stopped for breath and saw the twinkle in his eyes. She'd been had again.

With a wide grin, he turned back to the waitress, "Make that two banana cream pies. And hold the cottage cheese."

Despite herself, Quinn felt a giggle burbling up. Her father used to make her laugh like this. It felt good to laugh again and she had to admit Gabriel had really had her going. They still had one minor problem, however.

"Did you fail to notice there's only one piece left?" she asked.

"Nah. This is a restaurant, not my mother's kitchen.

They probably have a dozen more in the back.'' He dumped a heaping spoon of sugar into his cup.

"You think so?" Despite his prompt reassurances, she had her suspicions. Looking up, she caught his gaze. The intensity of his stare made her nervous.

"Odd combination," he said thoughtfully.

"I don't think so," she murmured, "lots of people like pie and coffee."

"Nah," his thick black hair swayed with the toss of his head. "I mean your name. Rosetti/Quinn. Italian/Irish. Strange."

"My folks didn't think it so strange," she responded archly.

"Sure. And some people like mayonnaise on ham sandwiches."

"*I* like mayonnaise on my ham sandwiches." She prodded her chest for emphasis with a polished nail.

"Knew you were odd," Gabe said as he spooned another helping of sugar into his cup. "With a combination like that, I'll bet you have a hell of a temper."

He sipped his coffee and added more sugar.

"Now, why would you say that?" she demanded, pulling the sugar bowl from his grasp. "Three spoonsful—it's a wonder you have any teeth left!"

"Well, with that Irish red hair and . . . everybody knows Italian women are temperamental, too. You got a double whammy." He yanked the sugar container back and added another dollop to his cup.

"I am not temperamental!" she shouted. "And you are the most judgmental, arrogant . . ." she broke off, noticing the interested stares of the patrons at the neighboring tables. "You make me crazy, you know that?" she hissed.

"You got a nerve," he whispered back, "calling me arrogant and judgmental. You took my sugar! Besides, what do you mean—it's a wonder I have any teeth left? Look, my teeth are fine, see . . ." he grinned widely, exposing even white teeth. He stuck his thumb and forefinger in his mouth as one might do in order to remove their dentures.

For one awful second she thought he was indeed going to take out a set of false teeth. In a subconscious gesture, she pulled her paper napkin up, covering the lower part of her face.

Then, with a broad wink, he removed his fingers and picked up the thick pottery cup and took a huge sip.

"Yuck! This is terrible, why'd you let me ruin my coffee?"

"Why did . . . I . . . *let* you . . ." she sputtered, incoherent at his accusation. As if she were in some way responsible for his actions.

"Yeah, I don't know how I'm going to trust you with the life of that unsuspecting cat, if you can't be responsible for one cup of coffee. Where'd you suppose that waitress is?"

Quinn rubbed her forehead with the tips of her fingers. She didn't understand it. She should have a headache by now. But she had to admit that he wasn't dull. She had never considered herself slow-witted, but his humor was so dry that she got sucked in time and again.

A smile snuck up on her mouth. Before she knew it, a giggle had found its way to her throat. It was impossible to stay angry with him. Even now, as her laughter welled at the surface and finally gushed in a free-spirited belly laugh, Gabriel maintained his innocent expression—as if he couldn't imagine what she found so amusing.

"Did I say something funny?" His dark brow arched quizzically.

"Mr. Hunter, I'm beginning to believe you've . . ." she had to stop and catch her breath, ". . . never had a serious moment in your life!"

"Oh, no," he said quickly. "Life is very serious, it's just my attitude toward it that's somewhat off-kilter."

His toffee colored eyes darkened as the waitress finally returned to place forks and napkins in front of them.

"Sorry to take so long, folks," she said as the flatware clattered to the counter. "Be right back with your pie. How 'bout a warm-up on that java?"

After she moved away, Gabriel continued. "I have this philosophy that we create our own destinies. And if we *perceive* the circumstances in our lives to be happy, then the very force of our positive energy causes that perception to become truth."

He stopped suddenly, looking somewhat abashed at his serious outburst. "Besides," he continued, with merriment again dancing in his eyes, "there's only one thing that makes me really grumpy."

"What's that?"

"When lovely ladies call me Mr. Hunter. Most people just call me Gabe."

"All right, Gabe." How strangely sweet his name tasted on her lips. It was a name not often heard anymore. Old-fashioned, yet with an innate honesty about it. A rugged, yet gentle sound.

She was interrupted from her ruminations when the waitress approached.

"I got some good news and some bad news, folks."

"What's the good news?" Gabe and Quinn asked in unison.

"Ah, a duet, that's nice." The waitress rubbed her hands on her lace-trimmed pink apron. "Well, the good news is we only got one piece of banana cream pie left."

Quinn and Gabe looked at one another in confusion. Gabe tapped the side of his head with the heel of his hand as if to clear his thoughts. "That was the good news?"

"Sure. Think of all them calories and fatty things you were talking about—now you don't have to worry about 'em."

"Oh, I see," he said in a tone that clearly indicated that he didn't, "Then what's the bad news?"

"That you two have to fight over who gets that last piece." With that, she sat the sumptuous wedge precisely between them on the Formica counter and walked off.

Gabriel poked the saucer with a forefinger. It moved a half inch in Quinn's direction. "You take it."

"No, that's okay," she pushed it back, "I really don't need it."

"I was only joking about the calories. One piece of pie isn't going to affect *your* figure." He eyed her appraisingly.

She felt hot under his close scrutiny. She'd been X-rayed with less intensity.

"Besides," he continued, oblivious to her discomfort, "you saw it first."

He nudged the saucer in front of her. The thick, foamy mound of whipped cream quivered from the movement. No, he wasn't going to be the only magnanimous one. She had self-control.

Squenching her eyes shut against the temptation, she shoved the plate back toward Gabriel. Unfortunately, she used a little more force than intended and the thick slab of pie slid off the china plate and onto the counter.

Oh, no. Not another fiasco, she groaned to herself, looking at the mess. Marla was always trying to read her biorhythmns—today Quinn should have relented.

With a nonchalant shrug, he licked the tip of his finger. "Do you remember the old Li'l Abner cartoon?"

She nodded, speechless with embarrassment. Maybe she ought to carry a banner warning passersby of danger.

Gabe continued. "There was a bit character in those cartoons, a Joe something or other. Always walked around with a dark cloud over his head and trouble followed him everywhere."

"A jinx." Unaccountably, she felt a lump in her throat. He thought she was a jinx. Bad luck. A walking disaster.

Gabe reached over and wiped a smudge of meringue from her chin with a paper napkin. He shook his head ruefully. "Well, since I met you, I feel like old Joe. I'm sorry, Quinn. Hope I didn't embarrass you."

She could have kissed him. Maybe he did have a little gallantry after all.

The buxom waitress appeared before them, a Pyrex coffee pot in hand. "We have a policy against pie throwing in here." She poured refills into their mugs. "Could I interest you in the coconut cream or how about the custard?"

Shaking their heads, they sat, eyes downcast like two naughty children, while the waitress cleaned the pie off of the counter.

"Some things just aren't meant to be," Gabe said mournfully, as they watched the waitress dump the thick, gooey mess into the garbage.

"Yes, I'm sure it was for the best," she added, thinking of those extra three pounds.

They sighed in unison.

"Well," Gabe said brightly, "I guess we really should discuss what we're going to do about the cat."

"Mmm-hmm," she agreed, still thinking about that pie. Why hadn't she eaten breakfast?

"I suppose alternating custody would be the best plan," he suggested.

"Sounds okay to me. You can have him first."

"Oh, no, really. You go ahead," he insisted.

"You're Elvira's relative, you take him first."

"Oh, no, I couldn't. You first. I insist."

They looked at each other, eyes narrowed like two fighters appraising their opponents. This politeness was going to end up being a danger to someone's health.

FOUR

Two hours later, Quinn settled into her old VW bug and prepared for the long drive into the mountains. She opened her handbag and riffled through the contents. Keys, wallet, sunglasses; the methodical check of her belongings consumed her mental energy and helped sort her emotions as well.

She felt as soggy as yesterday's hotcakes.

What a day, she thought, as she glanced at her wristwatch. Three-thirty? She shook her arm and held the watch to her ear. Tick . . . tick . . . it droned with steady monotony. Quinn couldn't believe it was so early. If her frazzled emotions were any indication, it should have been midnight.

Quinn felt as though she'd spent the day being battered by a hurricane. Gabe Hunter was not a restful person to be around. Still, he *was* interesting, she admitted, recalling his introduction to the large ginger cat, McLeish.

The moment Gabe opened the carrier, McLeish bounded out like a sprinter at the starting gun.

Gabe had gamely set after the elusive feline, but the cat wasn't about to be recaptured. Quite a chase scene had ensued through the lobby of Kresge, McGuire & Shaw, culminating with a race across the receptionist's desk.

Although Gabe had ultimately prevailed, McLeish had continued to hiss and snarl as he was recaged. Remembering the glazed expression on the young receptionist's face, Quinn imagined she had probably handed in her notice. Law offices were supposed to be staid and quiet.

She unloosened her heavy auburn hair from its knot, letting it tumble freely around her shoulders. With splayed fingers, she combed the strands and massaged her weary scalp. It didn't help much as the tension seemed to radiate down her neck. Quinn hunched and rotated her shoulders. She was so stiff! She felt as if she had been under pressure for days.

It was that Gabriel Hunter, the thought came unbidden into her mind.

Well, you just forget that idea, old girl, she chided herself. Just because the man was tall, dark, sexy, and had an outrageous sense of humor was no reason to lose her perspective. He was also schizo, she reminded herself.

Besides, the sobering reminder crept into her consciousness, her relationship with Gabriel Hunter had to remain strictly platonic. She had accepted a responsibility and she was bound to maintain her objectivity—in spite of his infectious grin.

Her fingers drummed the steering wheel as she waited for a green light. With each tap, she ticked off a reason to avoid him.

His mind was short-circuited.

Dippy sense of humor.

He was arrogant.

Immature.

Probably irresponsible.

Oh, she could think of dozens of reasons to steer clear of Mr. Hunter—if she hadn't agreed to do just the opposite.

So intent was she on cataloging Gabe's shortcomings, that she barely noticed as the scenery sped past. Her mind barely registered Rancho Bernardo, with its plethora of white stucco structures topped with red tile roofs. Suddenly, she noticed a green and yellow highway sign announcing the Lake Hodges exit. Escondido was just ahead.

Her heart raced at the appropriateness of the name. Spanish for hiding place, to Quinn it meant the comfort and security of her only living relation—her father.

Glancing in her rearview mirror to make sure she was clear of on-coming traffic, she quickly moved into the exit lane. Right now, what she needed more than anything was to see Pop.

A soft smile lit her face as she thought of her father. He'd really be surprised to see her on a Friday afternoon. Normally, Fridays were spent getting the shop ready to open Saturday morning. The small specialty shops of Idyllwild depended on the tourists for their survival and during the off-season were only open on weekends and holidays.

Although the shortened work week left Quinn ample time to work in her garden and craft her scarecrows, it certainly made for a slender income. It was far too expensive to run the utilities and pay help for the meager local trade during the week. But you had to gnaw pretty close to the bone on a two-day work week, only occasionally supplemented by teaching night classes at the local art institute.

Sometimes the pressure of trying to juggle the shop, her aged cabin, and Pop's nursing home expenses made her want to throw her belongings into the VW and drive until it ran out of gas. But her stressful worries usually dissolved when she went to see her father.

She would give anything to see him regain his mental clarity. He was quite a scamp in his youth, but since her mother's death, Daniel had faded until he was only a dim image of his former self.

She turned off Grand and headed for the older, tree-lined section of town. Stately rows of eucalyptus trees stood guard over a quaint mixture of Spanish stucco and early thirties frame houses.

Two blocks from the Shady Rest Convalescent Home, Quinn spotted the gleaming white of a See's candy store. Pop wasn't supposed to have sweets, but just one piece of his favorite, butternut caramel, couldn't possibly hurt.

She ran into the store and emerged moments later, clutching a small white bag. She'd only meant to buy one piece, but that seemed too piddling to bother with.

A stab of guilt gored her in the stomach. She'd done it again. Just like the old Quinn—buying and doing more for other people than they needed or wanted. Pop wouldn't appreciate her bringing him the candy; he probably wouldn't even recognize her.

Although it was like finding gold in the Dutchman's mine when her father was alert, he was still a comfort if all he did was to rock and smile blandly at the wall.

She pulled the car into the parking lot of the rest home, suddenly anxious to tell her father all about the disturbing events of her day. And one very disturbing man.

Crossing her fingers for luck, Quinn skipped up the brick stairs and into the polished tile lobby.

The nurse's station was vacant so she pushed the courtesy bell on the counter. While she waited, she tucked the white bag of candy deep into her purse. A moment later Mrs. Kingwalton, the head nurse, marched across the lobby—her stiff white uniform an audible tribute to the wonders of starch. Despite her drill-sergeant manner and adherence to procedure, Quinn knew her to be devoted to the welfare of her patients.

"Oh, Miss Rosetti, we didn't expect to see you today."

"I had some business in town and thought I'd drop by. How is he today?"

"Not bad today. Fed himself at lunch." Mrs. Kingwalton unpinned a pendulum watch from her bosom and frowned at it. "Only twenty more minutes 'til visiting hours are over. Must keep to the rules. Patients expect order, you know."

Quinn grimaced, remembering how much her father

loved spontaneity. Maybe it was a blessing there were gaps in his memory.

"May I stay and help with his dinner?"

The nurse's lower lip curled up over her top one. Her bass voice seemed to lose a layer of harshness. "Quinn, you know you can stay if you want. It's just . . . well, I wouldn't advise it."

"Why?" She was confused. Many relatives of other patients helped with their loved ones and the staff seemed to appreciate the relief. But for some reason, Quinn had never met much success when she'd offered to help with Daniel.

"Well, you know . . . your dad . . ." Nurse Kingwalton stumbled over her words. "Your dad isn't like most of the others. When he's alert, *all* of his faculties work, and he'd die of shame if he found out that you'd seen him unable to feed himself. No, t'would break his heart."

Clucking sorrowfully, she led the way to the sunroom. As the door swung open, a dozen pairs of eyes looked up expectantly. Then, recognizing Quinn, eleven seniors smiled, nodded weakly, and went back to waiting.

But one pair of deep brown eyes sparkled at the sight of her.

"Quinnie! My little monkey," Daniel Rosetti called, using a pet name from her childhood. "What a surprise. Come give your old dad a hug."

He turned to the other seniors and shouted, "Hey, everybody, say Hi to my daughter, Quinn. Ain't she a looker?"

The weathered faces smiled at the proud father. They had all met Quinn many times, but whenever Daniel was alert, he shouted an introduction. Quinn had long since gotten over her embarrassment. In fact, she sort of enjoyed his enthusiasm. There wasn't much to enjoy for most of these people.

"You look great today, Pop," she said, hugging him

warmly. He might be an old scoundrel, but his daughter adored him.

"Sit. Sit." He patted the cushion on the tweed sofa.

Though the staff tried to make the place bright and cheery, there was no escaping the institutional feeling of the visiting room. Faded stucco walls, serviceable furniture, and a dozen gentle old folks with confused minds. How she looked forward to bringing her father home.

"So, what brings you down the hill today, honey?"

Looking around for the indomitable Mrs. Kingwalton, she slipped the burgeoning paper bag to her father.

"You came all this way to bring me a caramel?" His eyes, alert and vibrant, assessed his daughter.

"No. . . ."

Daniel walked to the door and looked down the hallway. "Coast is clear," he announced, passing the bag of candy to old Mr. Taylor. Quickly, the white paper bag was passed around the room.

Quinn smothered a grin as she watched the seniors sucking on the sweets, looking for a moment like happy children. Suddenly, she was glad she had given in to the impulse to buy so much.

"So, tell your old man." Her father's booming voice interrupted her thoughts. "Problem at the shop?"

Slowly, hesitantly, Quinn told him of the day's events. She averted her eyes, skimming over her initial reaction to Gabe.

But this was one of Daniel Rosetti's good days—and he knew his daughter.

"So, this Hunter guy, real jerk, huh?"

"No . . . not really. Just takes a little getting used to."

"Yeah, I know the type." Daniel sucked on a piece of toffee. "Them guys are usually loud-mouth slobs. Big bellies—beer drinkers."

Quinn thought of Gabe's well-formed physique and smiled. "No, Pop, no beer gut."

"Disgusting personal habits?"

She laughed in spite of herself. Daniel's banter could always coax a smile from her. "Oh, Pop, of course not. It's just that he's . . . too good-looking, never serious, too smooth-talking . . ."

"Whew!" Daniel whistled. "Sounds like a psychopathic personality if I ever heard of one. Couldn't be, could it, that he reminds you just a little of David Simmons?"

"Oh, no," she objected, "he doesn't look at all like David." But she knew her father wasn't referring to Gabe's looks. She thought for a moment, then admitted, "In a way, maybe. That same kind of sophistication."

"Too much for a poor little country girl?" He raised a speculative brow.

Quinn shook her head and scowled. He was putting her on. Holding her insecurities up in front of her. Making her see for herself the absurdity of her prejudices.

"So, what else is wrong with him?" Daniel asked, a little too nonchalantly. He knew with his red-haired daughter, the direct approach didn't always work.

"Oh, Pop . . . I don't know. Yes, I do. He's crass and irresponsible and cocky and . . ." she stared at her hands, folded demurely in her lap, thumbs circling one another like a paddlewheel churning water.

Daniel gazed at his daughter, remembering her senior year when she'd stared lovingly at her rotating thumbs whenever Buzzy Keilor's name had been mentioned. Whatever happened to that boy, he wondered. He reached over and stroked her silky hair.

"Hmmmph. Really like him, huh?"

Quinn bowed her head and nodded at the ground. "But you don't understand. I have to keep my distance, otherwise I might lose my objectivity and . . ."

"Would that be so bad?"

"Yes! I mean, even if I ended up hating him, it would mean that I couldn't be impartial. I have to do the very best I can at this crazy job. Or else I can't accept Mrs. Featherstone's bequest.''

Daniel rubbed the stubble on his long, thin face. "Setting yourself up for a pretty big problem, aren't you?"

"No," she shook her head emphatically, "I've thought it over pretty carefully, and I think it's just a matter of telling the truth."

He patted his daughter's hand. "If there's one thing I regret in this life, Monkey, it's being responsible for you being so serious about everything. I know," he held up a hand to cut off her protest, "I know, I gave you a lot of love, but because I never grew up—you had to do it faster."

Mrs. Kingwalton's large form filled the doorway. "Visiting hours are up. Dinner time."

Daniel placed his thin arm around his daughter's shoulder. "Honey, I know I taught you to value truth and integrity above all else, but sometimes I think I forgot to teach you some other real important values."

They paused at the doorway as Quinn looked up at her father, a puzzled frown on her face. "I . . . I don't understand." Somehow, she was afraid of his words.

"Well, honey, it's one thing to seek truth and another to weigh it. Sometimes, our minds have a way of twisting all around something without seein' it straight on."

She shook her head, thoroughly confused. Although mostly self-educated, Daniel Rosetti was a well-read and learned man. On his good days, Quinn had a hard time keeping up with his agile mind.

He hugged her tight and brushed his lips against the top of her head. "Honey, a wise man by the name of Einstein said it better than I ever could. He said that when somebody undertakes to set himself up as a judge of truth and knowledge, that somebody is going to be shipwrecked by the laughter of the gods. Or words to that effect."

Daniel sighed, and kissed his only child on the top of

her head. "All I'm trying to tell you is, be careful of the whims of them gods."

Quinn chewed her lower lip. Her father's parting words had been confusing and strangely upsetting. He had made it sound like her reliance upon truth could be wrong! Lately, it seemed as if the very foundations of her character rested on shifting desert sands. Every time she looked down, her base had changed.

First, generosity had started backfiring and now it appeared that truth could be dangerous. The world suddenly seemed very complicated.

Still, it had been a good decision to stop. Just being with her father, even during his vague times, imbued her with a sense of familial belonging. She could certainly understand Elvira Featherstone's need to tighten her family ties in those last months before her death. A sense of sadness enveloped Quinn as she thought of the older woman, alone in her final years. When, God forbid, her pop finally fell victim to the vagaries of his illness, she, too, would be alone in the world.

Glancing out the car window at the tall pines and cedars flanking the roadside did little to lighten her melancholic mood. Their long, sad shadows reminded Quinn of the emptiness in her life. An unbidden picture of Gabe's crooked grin crept before her eyes as if he were the answer to her solitude.

Quinn insistently banished the vision to the darkest recesses of her mind. If there was anything she *didn't* need—it was him cluttering her life. She was just tired and overwrought from the emotion-filled day.

Finally, she saw Hurkey Creek Park on the right and knew home was only a few moments away. If only she didn't have to work tomorrow—the way she felt right now, she could crawl under Gramma's quilt and sleep for a week.

Shaking her head to chase away the weariness, Quinn

turned her concentration to the winding road. The last five miles were the worst as the road twisted and turned on itself like an angry snake. Her eyes were bleary and the sky had darkened to a deep sapphire blue.

Glancing into the deepening twilight, Quinn pressed harder on the gas pedal. A late fall storm was rapidly approaching. She loved the crackle and melodrama of thunderstorms—from the shelter of her living room. But years on the hill had provided many examples of the folly of driving in the torrential rain.

In the distance, a crack of thunder reverberated like the report from a rifle. To pass the time, she imagined lighting the fireplace and curling up with a glass of wine. But, again, the vision of Gabe Hunter intruded into her fantasy. This time he was sitting on the floor, leaning against her sofa—the firelight casting warm shadows on his golden eyes.

A sigh of relief escaped her throat as the sign announcing Strawberry Creek Road peeped through the gloom.

Ah, home. She smiled. Fire. A bowl of hot chili. Snuggling in her bunny p.j.s. Curling up with her favorite afghan and a good murder mystery. And without a single thought of Mr. Hunter, thank you.

Her mouth drooped in a frown. Yeah, that *would* be a nice way to spend the evening *after* two hours of stuffing and clothing scarecrows.

At last, sighing with fatigue, she turned into her driveway.

An hour later Quinn had showered, brushed her light auburn hair until it shone, and bundled in her jammies and robe. She stoked the fire and breathed in the dusky aroma of the smoldering logs, reminding her somehow of Gabe's subtle masculine scent.

Now, stop it! she chided herself, as she gave the wood a sharp poke. A shower of red needles flew upward and the heat rose, kissing her already flaming cheeks. Darn it! She was *not* going to think about that man again tonight.

To strengthen her resolve, she turned her attention to

building the perfect fire. She crumpled a sheet of newspaper and stuck it in the corner where the fire hadn't yet taken hold. Reaching for another page, she noticed it was the cartoon section. Running her finger down the page, she found Snoopy dressed in his raincoat and fedora, pecking at an ancient typewriter from atop his dog house. Woodstock perched on his shoulder, admiring his pal's prose.

It was a dark and stormy night, the feckless beagle had written.

A white flash jagged through the windows, quickly followed by the thwack of thunder. Somehow her stormy night seemed more imposing than Snoopy's, accentuating this new feeling of loneliness.

Then a grumble from her neglected stomach reminded her of that bowl of spicy chili she had promised herself. The scarecrows could wait. Few tourists would venture up the mountain in this heavy rain so she probably had enough stock on hand.

Setting the brass poker back on its stand, she started for the kitchen when someone pounded on the front door.

Who on earth? Marla usually devoted Friday nights to studying and a neighbor would have either called first or honked at the foot of the driveway to announce their arrival.

Another crack of thunder—close—caused the lights to flicker. Her heart dropped to her stomach and raced back, its pounding echoing the steady thump-thump on her front door. There was an ominous feeling in the air and she remembered a fragment of something she had once read about evil lurking in dark places.

She snapped on a table lamp, feeling slightly silly. Burglars rarely announced their arrival by knocking. Still, it never hurt to be prepared. Retrieving the fireplace poker, she padded across the room.

The pounding had stopped and a dead silence claimed the air.

She peeked around the corner at the oval of etched glass in the front door.

Darn, she hadn't turned the porch light on, only a vague shadow wavered behind the frosted glass.

"Who . . . who's there?" she squeaked.

The only response was a renewed banging, causing the heavy door to quaver on its hinges. Quinn clutched the heavy iron bar with trembling fingers as a slash of brilliant blue lightning lit the small area.

It was a dark and stormy night, the cartoon dog whispered in her ear. "Thanks, Snoopy," she muttered. "You're the one who started this."

"Quinn? Quinn is that you?" A muffled male voice called from the porch. Although eerie in the electric air, there was a familiar quality to it.

She inched closer to the frosted glass.

"Quinn, stop kidding around, will ya? It's starting to rain."

Gabriel Hunter. Recognition slammed into her and for some peculiar reason, her heart hammered anew.

Oh no, she moaned as she looked down at her flannel nightwear. And no mascara. Giving in to those whimsical gods Daniel had warned her about, she shrugged and gave her hair a cursory pat. As Pop always said, "drop-in company has to be satisfied with pot-luck."

Dropping the poker into an umbrella stand, she dusted her hands on her flannel robe and unlatched the door.

"It's about time," Gabe filled the doorway and stepped across the sill, as if invited.

"What are you doing here, and what's *that?*" She suddenly noticed the large white cat carrier firmly clasped in his right hand.

"You know perfectly well that's McLeish." He set the carrier on the floor, slipped off a corduroy jacket and pushed a damp strand of black hair from his eyes.

"I know what it is—I just want to know why it's here," she snapped as she hung his coat on the antique hall tree.

Just for an instant, she held onto the jacket, enveloping her senses in the unique musky aroma that was Gabe.

"Don't call him an it; you'll hurt his feelings. Huh, guy?" Gabe murmured soothingly to the animal as he bent over to unlatch the cage door.

"What are you doing here?" she repeated.

"Bringing you McLeish," he said in a matter-of-fact tone. "Got any coffee?"

"Are you trying to tell me that you drove a hundred miles for cof . . . what do you mean bringing *me* the cat?" Her dark eyes narrowed with suspicion.

"Well, I have a small problem." Gabe stuck his hand inside the cage and emerged with a fat, snarling mass of ginger fur. "Atta boy." He rubbed the back of the cat's head.

McLeish responded to his kindness by biting his forefinger.

"Ouch! This cat hates me." He dropped the animal to the floor and stuck his finger in his mouth. McLeish edged toward the open doorway.

"This cat is only one of many," she said, reaching around him to shut the front door.

McLeish shook himself to plump out his long fur and looked around belligerently. Although Quinn knew him to be a pampered house cat, he looked as if he had survived many an alley brawl. His face was so flat, it looked indented. One ear stood straight up, the other was crimped at the tip. A small crescent-shaped scar over one eye gave him a perpetual look of bored contempt.

Shaking his head, he gave Quinn a flat-faced glare and strolled majestically into the living room to survey this new remote outpost of his kingdom.

McLeish was one bad dude.

"No, I'm serious," Gabe insisted, sucking his finger between words. "This guy is homicidal. Got any merthiolate?"

"In the bathroom," she pointed down the hall.

"Aren't you going to help? I can't just go grubbing

around in a strange bathroom . . .'' His pale eyes flickered in dismay or amusement—she couldn't tell which.

Dropping her arms to her sides in a gesture of submission to the fates, she followed him down the hall.

Quinn flipped on the bathroom light fixture and pointed to the commode. "Have a seat."

Gabe complied and looked around. "Hey, that's great—an old claw-foot tub. Boy, they sure knew how to make 'em back then."

"Mmm-hmm," she responded, rummaging through the medicine cabinet and finally extracting a dusty bottle of iodine.

"Yeah," he continued, running his hand over the curved porcelain edge, "these babies were one of the prime reasons that marriages lasted so long in the olden days. Did you know that?"

"No," she answered flatly, as she ran hot water over the iodine lid. That top probably hadn't been off in ten years. She wondered if iodine could go bad. Maybe, she thought hopefully as the cap finally twisted free, maybe its potency *increased* with age.

"Yep," Gabe slapped the tub with his palm. "Bathtubs built for two and beds built for one. Those people understood togetherness."

"Hold still. Let me see," she said, choosing to ignore the thrust of his conversational gambit. Already, being confined with him in such a small space made her feel claustrophobic.

Taking his large hand in both of her own, she looked for teethmarks. She scanned his palm, then turned it over and looked at the top. "I don't see anything."

"What! Are you blind? Look at that." He pointed indignantly to a reddish pinprick in a crease of his index finger.

Quinn clasped her hand to her heart. "Oh, my God. Take it away. I can't bear to look. There was so much mutilation during the war—I can't stand any more."

"Smart aleck," he muttered. "Just put the merthiolate on."

With more than a little righteous glee, she smeared the iodine across his finger.

"Ouch. Ow. Burns. You cheated," he yelped in mock pain. "Blow. Blow." He held his painted finger in front of her mouth.

Quinn puckered and blew one short breath in the general direction of Gabe's finger. "Okay, baby, Mommy's through."

Holding his injured finger to his mouth, Gabe continued to blow. "Does this mean I get my coffee now?"

Quinn faced him, fists on her slender hips. "Provided I get an explanation. Deal?"

"Deal," he agreed, following her to the kitchen.

Keeping up a non-stop flow of one-liners, mostly about his job, Gabe helped make the coffee. ". . . so, the guy sends a telegram to his buyer. He's trying to save money wherever he can, so he uses his own shorthand system. You know, fewer words—less money for the telegram. So anyway, the telegram says: Suspend order. 5,000 missing. So what does the buyer do? You'll never believe this, the guy buys five thousand pairs of suspenders!"

Pushing back tears of laughter, Quinn grabbed her stomach and begged, "Enough! Please. Here, hand me the cream from the fridge."

She set two steaming mugs on the kitchen table and sat down across from him. "Okay. Enough jokes. So, what's the story? You've had time to come up with a good one by now."

Gabe shook his head, caramel eyes wide with innocence. "Story? Me? No way. It just never occurred to me that my tenant's association wouldn't allow cats."

"I see," she said, sipping her coffee. "So, you want me to take over your . . . responsibility?"

"No, of course not." He patted her hand, as if to

reassure her of his honorable intentions. "I'll do my share. It's just that . . ."

She sat back and stared into his eyes. Another one. Give it to Quinn—she'll do anything. Well, this time he was wrong. Her days of being a fish to be hooked by any sob story were over. Besides, it wouldn't be fair to deprive him of this opportunity for character growth. Taking care of helpless creatures taught responsibility and it was obvious he needed a good dose of that!

She measured her words carefully. "Just what do you consider to be your share. Don't tell me. Let me guess. Let's see, you were going to offer to pay for his food, if I took care of him, right? Wrong, mister."

She was getting warmed up to her subject now. This was, after all, the new Quinn.

Setting her mug carefully on the table, she leaned over and shook her forefinger at him. "In the first place, this is a fifty-fifty deal and I intend to see that you have the full benefit of your fifty percent. I don't know where people like you get the nerve to think that everyone else is just going to jump in and take over for you whenever something becomes inconvenient. Well, I'm putting you on notice, mister, that . . ."

"Damnation!" Gabriel slammed the flat of his hand on the table. "Enough already! I wasn't asking you to donate a vital organ."

"Why not?" she countered, dark eyes flashing. "You'd be perfectly willing to allow me the honor—I'm sure."

"For your information," he pointed his finger at her, but somehow the threat was lessened by the iodine stain, "I didn't come here to ask you to take over completely; only to change our agreement enough to allow me time to move into a new apartment—one that would let me keep him."

McLeish, as if realizing he was the subject of their conversation, wandered back into the room and began investigating every nook.

"You . . . you mean," she stammered, taken aback by this new dimension of him, "that you'd actually *move* so you could take your turn?"

"Yes, although I don't know why the ingrate deserves it," he shook his head.

"Mrrrow!" McLeish protested the slanderous remark and sailed out of the room, tail erect like a signal flag.

Quinn got up and fetched the coffee pot to stall for time. Maybe she had misjudged him. No, more likely he had made that up on the spur of the moment when he saw she wasn't going to fall for his ploy.

She was saved from having to decide as the entire kitchen lit up at the same time a thunderous crack pealed from nearby. Although she was used to the violent storms, the strike was so close that Quinn jumped from her seat with an audible gasp. The lighting flickered again.

Gabe patted her hand soothingly. "It's okay. Really. My other great-aunt, Ibbie, used to say the Lord just bowled another strike."

After a moment Quinn's heart stopped pounding. That one had been close. For some curious reason, she was comforted by Gabe's presence.

"All right," she said as she poured more coffee, "how long will it take you to move?"

He took a sip. "Well, I gave my thirty-days' notice. So, I thought that instead of each of us taking a week that you could keep him for a month, then I'd take him."

Theoretically, there was no fault with his solution, but it would certainly be a detriment to her underlying problem. How could she observe him for the two months if he was in the city and she was on the mountain? Still, how could she object without revealing her dilemma?

A frantic meowing from the living room interrupted her train of thought.

"Oh, poor baby. He's probably afraid of the storm."

"Hmmph. More likely Mother Nature's afraid of him,"

Gabe grumbled, checking his finger as they started for the living room.

Unfortunately, Gabe's prediction turned out to be more correct. As they stepped into the living room, McLeish was engaged in mortal combat with Oscar, one of Quinn's favorite scarecrows. For two years Oscar had lived a quiet life in the corner by the hearth. Now, his papier-mâché head lolled and his straw innards were scattered over the carpet.

Oscar had been no match for the feisty ginger cat.

"Oh, no," Quinn moaned.

McLeish turned at the sound, a clump of straw clutched in his mouth.

His rump a-swagger, he marched across the room and presented Quinn with a tribute of his victory as he dropped the soggy wad of straw at her feet.

"Oh poor Oscar," she wailed. It was stupid, she knew, but she felt a lump in her throat as she stared at the mutilated remains of the limp figure. Oscar was the first scarecrow she'd crafted. Inspired by her childhood nickname, she had fashioned Oscar into an organ grinder's monkey—complete with fez and tin cup.

McLeish was contentedly munching on the tassel prized from the mangled fez.

She crossed the room and picked up Oscar's dilapidated three-foot frame and started shoving handfuls of straw inside his shirt.

"Bad boy, McLeish. Bad boy," Gabe admonished the feline bully as he picked up straws from the carpet. "I'm sorry, Quinn. I should have warned you. This guy is trouble with a capital T."

"He's just lonely," she murmured, brushing a tear from her cheek. "He's confused and looking for affection. He used to have Mrs. Featherstone's full attention and now he's been confined to a kennel."

Gabe handed her the straw and a torn piece of Oscar's shirt sleeve. "Yeah, maybe. But until he makes his adjustment you've got to watch him every minute. In five minutes at my place he destroyed two magazines and an asparagus fern."

Quinn clutched Oscar to her breast. "But I have to work on the weekend. I can't let him run loose in the house. He'll destroy it."

"Lock him in the bathroom," Gabe suggested.

"How will he ever learn to adjust if I keep him confined?"

"Hmm. I don't know. How about if you left him outside?"

"He doesn't know this area. Elvira lived across town. He'll get lost or hit by a car. No, there's got to be a better . . ." she stopped abruptly as a flash of inspiration struck.

"What?" His dark brow raised quizzically.

"You can baby-sit while I work."

"Me? I hate to break this to you, but I earn a living, too."

"Sure," she agreed, "during the week. But the Scarecrow Emporium is only open on Saturdays and Sundays this time of the year, so you can watch him on the weekend and I'll be here the rest of the time. Simple."

"Simple?" he asked skeptically. "Are you suggesting that I rent a motel room for himself and me every weekend? Or maybe we can just sleep in my car?"

"Do you have to make everything such a monumental problem? I'm sure we can think of something." She tapped the side of her head with her forefinger as if to jog an idea loose.

Suddenly, Gabe snapped his fingers. "Got it! I'll stay with you."

"Oh, no, you don't," her sheaf of auburn hair shook emphatically. "I have enough problems with a quarrelsome cat."

"Don't tell me you're worried about what your boyfriend will say?" he goaded.

"I don't *have* a boyfriend," she snapped, then instantly regretted her quick response. Great going, she thought; he offers her a perfect out and her big mouth muffs it.

"Oh, you don't. Well then I think it's a perfect solution." As if he considered the matter settled, Gabe plumped down on the sofa, kicked off his shoes and propped his feet on the coffee table. "Have you eaten yet? I'm starved."

Quinn hugged Oscar as the rainstorm finally broke. Great plopping drops lashed against the window as a fresh spate of thunder and lightning reverberated through the house. She stared at Gabriel through the flicking light. The dancing flames illuminated his sardonic grin.

A strong premonition washed over her as she gazed at his strong features. Somehow, a new chapter in her life was beginning. She didn't know whether this chapter would be comic or tragic, but she couldn't ignore the sense of foreboding that told her her safe little existence would never be the same.

It was indeed a dark and stormy night.

FIVE

Quinn put out her hand as if to stop his words. "I don't think that's such a good idea."

Gabe's dark brow raised like raven's wings, ready to take flight. "Oh, afraid?"

"Of what?" she retorted, pointing a finger to the fireplace poker. "I can keep the likes of you in line."

Gabe winked and raised a questioning finger. "Ah, but the danger is—will you want to? Keep me in line, I mean."

She rolled her eyes. "Puh-lease. Don't flatter yourself."

"Then what's the problem?" He spread his arms wide, in a disarming gesture.

"The problem is, I don't know anything about you. And I'm not in the habit of letting strange men sleep in my house."

"How about not-so-strange men?" he countered.

She crossed the room and flopped onto the leather recliner in the corner. "That's juvenile, you know. Every time the subject turns the least bit serious, you crack a joke."

"Pardon *me*." He dropped onto the sofa and crossed his arms. "Next time you want to get serious, I'll just slit my wrists."

"See! You did it again."

He shook his head mournfully though his golden eyes glittered with humor. "Most people wouldn't consider slicing your wrists funny. You have a sick sense of humor."

Quinn couldn't think of a suitable rejoinder so she settled on a murderous glare.

Gabe sat up straight and slapped his palms on the coffee table. "Okay, you want serious? Serious you got. My life is an open book—ask me anything?"

She could think of a hundred questions. But the first one to touch her lips was a total surprise to her as well. "Wouldn't Mrs. Hunter mind you sleeping over every weekend?"

"There is no Mrs. Hunter," he said quietly, serious at last. "At least not any longer."

"Oh?" She didn't know what to say. She had expected him to be flip, not answer in such a grave tone.

"We divorced a couple of years ago."

"I'm sorry." *Liar*.

"Don't be. Tiffany's gone on to more, shall we say, golden pastures. Actually, I felt kind of sorry for her. Didn't get what she expected when she married me."

"What do you mean?"

He gave a rueful laugh. "She thought because I drove a fancy red Porsche and had a nice condominium at the beach that she was getting someone with mega-bucks."

"Are you saying she only married you for money?"

"My pride wants to think not. We had a couple of good years. And after all, it was my fault as much as it was Tiffany's."

Quinn looked up in surprise. David Simmons had *never* admitted any responsibility for their failed relationship. "How so?" she asked.

Gabe rubbed his chin thoughtfully. She could see the faint blur of razor stubble. Endearing, somehow. It gave a measure of vulnerability to the normally firm planes of his jaw.

Finally he turned, giving her the full impact of his tiger eyes, now dark with remembered pain. "It was my fault as much as hers because I changed course. When we first met I was a high-charged executive, storming the corporate ladder. Twelve-hour work days. Business dinners. Weekend golf meetings. There was no time to be Gabe Hunter. But somewhere down the road I realized that I'd rather be a human than CEO of a Fortune 500 company."

Quinn shook her head, her brow furrowed in sympathy. She'd never been a workaholic to that degree, but she *had* been trapped in the L.A. rat race for a while. She shuddered. "I know what you mean. That pace will kill you. So, you wanted to slow down—your . . . wife," she stumbled over the title, "didn't?"

"Ex-wife," he quickly amended. "No, let's just say Tiffany's parents gave her an apropos name. Tiffany wanted everything to be sterling—no silverplate. When she found out that I'd bought the condo just before the real estate market skyrocketed, and that I saved for two years for a down payment on the Porsche . . . and that we probably never would have a mansion in the Golden Triangle, well, it didn't take her long after that to realize she'd made a major mistake."

Quinn wanted to soothe his injured pride. Salve the hurt that was so apparent in his black-fringed eyes. She could certainly understand what it felt like to be used. But her own pride wouldn't let her tell him about David's betrayal, so she changed the subject.

"So, how were you related to Mrs. Featherstone?"

He smiled as if grateful that she'd dropped the subject of his former marriage. "Elvira was my grandfather's sister."

"Oh? Isn't it strange that Elvira would leave her estate to you instead of your father?" No sooner had the words left her lips that Quinn realized how tactless they sounded. She started to apologize, but he held up his hand.

"No, that's okay. I told you to ask anything. And Aunt Elvira didn't disinherit my mother. She left her a pretty sizable chunk. But since my folks aren't hurting for money, I guess she picked me for some unknown reason. I wish I'd known her better, done more for her when she was alive. I really liked the old girl, though." He smiled as if reliving a pleasant memory.

"Yes," Quinn agreed. "She was pretty special."

"So." Gabe stood up and bounced on his tiptoes. "Did I pass inspection?"

Closing her eyes, she cursed herself for a fool, and said, "I guess so. But remember, no funny stuff. And that— animal is your responsibility."

McLeish raised his head and wrinkled his nose. With a huge yawn, he demonstrated his opinion of their coversation, and dropped back onto his paws. A few seconds later, his lusty snore filled the air.

Quinn, too, rose to her feet and yawned. She was exhausted. This had to have been one of the most emotionally-charged days she'd had in years.

"Follow me," she said, "and I'll show you where the guest room is."

"You don't have a spare toothbrush, do you?"

"In the medicine chest."

"And do you shower in the morning or at night?"

"Why?"

"Because," he said, following on her heels down the hall, "if we're going to be roomies, we need to get all these details sorted out. Like who does the grocery shopping. And do I wash or dry? And laundry—I hope you do the laundry because I ruin something every week."

"Don't push it, Hunter." With a stern glare, she opened the door of the guest room and snapped on the overhead light.

"Brrrr. It's cold in here. Sure you don't want to help me stay warm?"

"Do I have to fetch the poker?"

"Just asking. Just asking." He held his hands out, palms up, as if to say she couldn't blame him for trying.

"Goodnight, Hunter," she said firmly.

She heard him chuckling long after she closed her own bedroom door.

Quinn awoke with a feeling of uneasiness. She hadn't slept well; a vague, nagging worry had kept intruding in her dreams.

It was because *he* was in her house.

In the scant twenty-four hours since Gabriel Hunter had stalked into her life with his long-legged stance and black-lashed eyes, Quinn's well-ordered existence had been turned inside out. Gabe invaded every minuscule aspect of her life. If she wasn't arguing with him, she was thinking about him. If she wasn't harnessing her raging hormones, she was dreaming about him.

Damn the man!

The room was still dark. It'd been ages since she'd wakened before dawn. Especially during a rainstorm. A good battering storm was usually a welcome friend, but last night's downpour had felt like Chinese water torture on her already taut nerves.

She nuzzled deeper in the bed, tucking the comforting warmth of the quilt under her chin as she tried again to find the solace of sleep.

It was no use. The creak of the guest room bed brought a fresh awareness of the man whose presence was like a raging river, reshaping the course of her life.

Her eyes snapped open. What was she doing, lying here mentally relinquishing control of her life to a near stranger? True, Gabe exuded a powerful magnetism and she felt like a tiny metal filing, drawn inexorably to his strength. Okay, so he was incredibly sexy and her ravenous body betrayed her with every thought and glimpse of him. So what?

So, she'd just ignore those raging hormones and go on with her normal routine. Gabe was a temporary aberration, in a couple of months he'd be gone from her life. In fact, he'd be gone from her home by Monday. All she had to do was concentrate on her work.

Her workshop was filled with half-finished scarecrows. Certainly enough to keep her errant mind occupied with thoughts other than the infuriating Mr. Hunter.

With the holiday season fast approaching, she and Marla had spent a tiddly afternoon inventing Christmas-Crows. So far, she had made a kelly-green elf and a rotund Santa; and this morning would give her the time to put the finishing touches on a bright-blue wooden soldier.

Fastening the top snapper of her bunnie jammies against the early morning chill, Quinn padded down the hall.

As she passed the guest room, a sudden noise caused her heart to jump. A strange, rumbling sound. Not particularly unpleasant . . . like a machine left on.

A quick smile curved her lips as she finally recognized the odd sound. Gabe was snoring.

Her hand seemed to move of its own volition as she twisted the knob and carefully eased the door open. She stood for a moment just inside the doorway. There was a curious intimacy implied in listening to a man snore. An intimacy she had no right to share.

Suddenly abashed at having invaded his privacy, Quinn started to leave the room when Gabe's snore grew abruptly louder. Then ceased abruptly.

The room was as silent as an old tomb.

Why had he stopped snoring? Was he awake? Quinn waited for one of his smart remarks but the room was ominously still. She had a sense of a hunter stalking his prey.

The best thing to do, she decided, was opt for an orderly retreat. With that end in mind, she turned around and started for what she hoped was the general direction of the bedroom door.

At that moment, her foot stepped on something squishy. And alive. McLeish let out a shriek that could have been heard by his relatives in the Himalayas. With an indignant swipe of his paw, he embedded his claws in the soft fabric of Quinn's pajama leg, relieving her of several layers of skin in the process. She added a yelp to the pre-dawn stillness.

"Jumping Jeminy Jehosaphat!" Gabe's irate voice thundered in the darkness. "What in the hell is going on?"

With a click, he turned on the bedside lamp, bathing the room in its bright glow. For an instant, silence reigned as everyone blinked in visual adjustment to the harshness of the sudden light.

McLeish adjusted first. Unfurling his claws from Quinn's p.j.s, he gave her ankle a contemptuous slap with his injured tail and sauntered out of the bedroom.

Rubbing the sleep from her eyes, she wondered how she was going to explain prowling around in Gabe's room while he was sleeping. Well, really it was her room, she amended, but he was using it. Somehow that didn't make the explanation seem any easier.

She cleared her throat and looked at Gabriel for the first time.

His sleep-tousled hair formed an ebony frame around his face giving him a soft, almost vulnerable look.

In startling contrast to his nudity.

Quinn felt a hot red flush begin in her toes and stretch upward until her entire body was sheathed in its fiery glow. But she couldn't take her eyes off of the tanned beauty of his muscular body. The broad expanse of lightly furred chest tapering down to a trim waist, amazingly bronze against the white sheets curled up in a wad beneath him.

She knew she was staring, but she couldn't seem to loosen her riveted stare from his flagrant masculinity.

"To what," his voice penetrated the fog that seemed to surround her, "do I owe the honor of this unexpected visit?"

Like a small, helpless animal entranced by a larger predator, Quinn lifted her gaze to his hypnotic eyes. "I . . . I didn't mean to wake you. I . . . just . . ." She raised her hands like a supplicant, but then, unable to explain, let them drop to her sides. She didn't understand why she felt so numb and unable to function. It wasn't as if she had never seen a naked man before. But her nerve endings were alive, dancing to a rhythm as ancient as time.

It was really this basic when you came down to it, she thought. Man. Woman. Mmmmmmph. Her blood rushed through her veins like molten lava coursing down a mountain.

Gabe sat up and rested nonchalantly on one elbow, apparently unconcerned with the effect his attire—or a lack thereof—was having on Quinn. Lifting a sleek, black eyebrow, he patted an empty space on the mattress beside him. "Come on in, plenty of room."

Had her desire been that obvious? She would have to be on guard every moment. His fiery gaze seemed to capture every nuance of her soul. Even now, his eyes swept the length of her body, their heat incinerating her protective clothing, leaving her feeling exposed and vulnerable.

Wrapping her arms tightly across her breasts, as if to protect herself from his blistering stare, she retorted, "Don't flatter yourself. I have better things to do with my time."

"Oh, I think I could manage to fill your time quite satisfactorily." The atmosphere crackled with vibration as his rejoinder filled the air, sounding more like an invitation than a challenge.

His words were like heat-seeking missiles, aimed for her and finding their target in her heated flesh and pounding heart. Quinn held her breath, afraid to move less her traitorous feet propelled her to the bed, into Gabe's waiting arms.

For a long moment they stayed quiet, eyes locked in a fierce battle of yearning so strong that they instinctively knew that neither would emerge unscathed. The air between them seemed to waver, radiating and expanding with the heat being generated by the two combatants.

Then, somewhere in the distance, a crowing rooster announced the sun's arrival and the magical moment dissolved as dawn lightened the room.

"So," Gabe announced abruptly, with an odd croak in his voice, "you never told me. What brings you here?"

Quinn shook her jumbled copper curls, still unable to speak for the violent pounding of her heart.

Gabriel tilted his head, and raised a jagged dark brow in the manner she had come to recognize as his cocky mood.

"Well, fair maiden, if you've come for an early morning tête-à-tête . . . I'm afraid one of us is severely overdressed for the occasion."

Quinn felt as though a bucket of ice water had been dumped on her overheated psyche. This was Gabe Hunter, remember? Del Mar's answer to Chevy Chase.

If for any reason the atmosphere turned the least bit serious—he turned on the wisecracks. Whatever had made her believe that he would have felt the electricity frissoning through the air? It was really unfair on her part, she reasoned, to expect sensitivity from him.

She remembered a time in grade school when a favorite teacher had determined that she should be right-handed instead of left. For months the teacher had coaxed, cajoled, and threatened. Finally, she had resorted to guilt: "Quinn, I had expected more effort from you."

So, Quinn had tried. Really tried. But she had only succeeded in disappointing both herself and the teacher. Quinn was meant to be a lefty. And Gabriel Hunter was meant to be irresponsible and frivolous.

But understanding didn't lessen the hurt and she could feel the sting of tears brighten her eyes. How could she have misread the man so badly? Elvira Featherstone had made a big mistake in relying on Quinn's judgment.

Pushing the hurt and confusion aside to be tested later like a sore tooth, she said tartly, "I imagine it's early for you, but the cat wants to go out. Coffee will be ready in ten minutes, if you want some."

"My, my, did we get up on the wrong side of the bed," Gabe chided as he slipped his arm through a shirt-sleeve. Although he had pulled the sheet around his hips, his long legs were still enticingly bare.

She eased toward the door, wanting to put space between her bruised ego and his flippancy.

"Leaving so soon? I thought we were just getting acquainted," his biting sarcasm reverberated through the quiet room.

Quinn stopped in the doorway, her hand clutching the frame. It wouldn't do to let him see that he had gotten to her. There would be no end to the teasing and ridicule if he saw a softening in her. She closed her eyes for a moment, summoning an appropriate putdown.

She turned back toward the bedroom. Gabe stood in the soft glow of the table lamp, the tan vee of his chest dark against the half-buttoned shirt. He had donned a pair of white jockey shorts that gleamed against his flat, dark abdomen. Nonchalantly, keeping his eyes firmly fixed on hers, he reached for his slacks.

Slowly, deliberately Quinn ran her eyes over his body. Raising her gaze to his face, she cocked an eyebrow contemptuously. "I was only windowshopping. Didn't see a *thing* worth buying."

She stepped out into the hallway and pulled the door behind her. Her heart was pounding in her chest. Never in her whole life had she been deliberately cruel to anyone. He looked so stunned Quinn felt like she had been kicking baby chicks. He would probably never get over her scathing comment. Men took things like that to heart. She had probably just destroyed that man's confidence.

A cold flush spread over her skin as she leaned against the wall. Maybe she should go back and apologize. But would that only encourage him to continue his barrage of one-liners?

As she pondered the problem and tried to salve her conscience, she became aware of another strange sound emitting from the guest room.

Curiosity overcoming good sense, Quinn grasped the door handle and inched it open.

Gabe stood in front of the dresser, running a brush

through the dark thatch of hair. He had to stoop to see into the mirror and his reflection was clear as Quinn peeked through the gap in the open door.

Poor destroyed Gabe Hunter was laughing.

Quinn released the door handle like it had suddenly caught fire. He didn't even have enough sensitivity to know he'd been insulted—cut to the core!

She stalked to the kitchen—murder, mayhem, and mangling on her mind. Had she taken complete leave of her senses, feeling an attraction to that man? Genghis Khan had been a sweet-talking feminist compared to Gabriel Hunter.

But that was okay—he who laughs last, and all of that. She'd have her revenge when it came time to submit Mr. Hunter's evaluation. Oh, yes, this would definitely be a factor.

She ran water into the coffeemaker and yanked eggs out from the fridge. Sure Rosetti, she chided herself, now fix the jerk breakfast—he'll appreciate it.

Keeping up a running commentary on his lackings, Quinn sliced sausage patties and scrambled eggs. She slung a red and white checked dishtowel over her shoulder— wishing she knew something about martial arts so she could sling Gabe across the room. That would wipe the crooked grin off his face. Calm started easing through her body as she gently stirred the eggs, visualizing his shocked expression if she were to suddenly heave him over her shoulder the next time he made a smart-aleck remark.

Her pleasant ruminations were suddenly interrupted by a soft mewing sound.

McLeish strolled into the kitchen, his tail a flagpole, stately waving from side to side. His dignified gait would have been convincing if not for the tufts of straw protruding from his mouth.

Oh no, she groaned, what had he destroyed now?

"Hunter," she bellowed, lungs straining with the force of her yell, "come take care of this cat!"

His voice directly behind her made her jump. "I'm on the same mountain—you don't have to shout. You really are nasty in the morning, aren't you?"

Without waiting for a retort, he scooped the ginger cat into his arms. Lowering his brows in a concerned manner, he spoke softly like someone attempting to pacify an escaped maniac. "We're going for some air. You should have some coffee or something. Calm yourself down."

He closed the kitchen door softly behind him.

Quinn threw the dishtowel across the room. She was *not* a hysterical person. Her life had been calm and orderly before he had come loping into her life with his long-legged stride.

There was a light tapping on the glass insert in the kitchen door.

Pulling aside the blue calico curtain, she saw Marla's shock of red hair.

They shared an easy-going friendship, but Marla had never before come visiting at 6:30 in the morning. With a queasy feeling of impending disaster, she opened the door.

"Who was that hunk? Oh, Quinn you've been holding out on your best buddy. To think I believed you! Going to town on business, Marla—monkey business, if you ask me. I can't believe you would keep something like that under wraps and . . ."

"Marla, stop for air. You're going to pass out," Quinn interrupted her friend's monologue and placed a mug of coffee in her hand. "Sit."

"Okay, but . . ."

"No buts," Quinn interjected. "I haven't had my coffee yet. No interrogation until I do."

Marla's pale face was flushed with agitation. "But I'm only trying to tell you . . ."

". . . tell me later. Can't you see I'm trying to . . . oh, no, my eggs are burning!"

She grabbed the dishtowel from the counter, wrapped it around the skillet handle, and pulled the pan from the flame. The scrambled eggs had the consistency of black rubber hip boots and were approximately the same color.

"I tried to tell you," Marla blew on her steaming mug, "but you kept interrupting."

A shaft of cold air swept through the room as the door opened. Gabe and McLeish stepped into the room and both sniffed the air, trying to identify the acrid odor. McLeish shook his head, licked a paw in disdain, and sauntered out of the kitchen.

Leaning over Quinn's shoulder, Gabe stared at the burned mess. He rubbed the small of her back, causing a rippling current to course through her body. With a slight shake of his head, he muttered, "No, thanks, really I don't eat breakfast. I'll just have toast."

He grabbed a mug from the rack. "Where's the sugar, sugar?"

Then, seeing Marla's wide-eyed stare, he hooked one foot around a chair leg and pulled it from the table. Gently easing his large frame into the chair, he stuck out his hand and said brightly, "Hi, Gabe Hunter. And you're . . . ?"

Marla squeaked out her name, clearly overwhelmed by the situation.

"So, Quinn, where'd you say the sugar was?"

Quinn thumped the sugar bowl onto the table. "You two might have all morning to drink coffee and gab, but *I* have things to do. *I* don't have all morning to sit around engaging in idle gossip. *I* have work to do. If you'll both excuse me?"

The plastic-soled feet of her pajamas scuffled along the bare wood floors as she made her way to the workroom. With her frazzled nerves, it took all of her concentration to balance the brimming mug of coffee.

Setting the mug on the scarred surface of her workbench, Quinn sank back onto her high-backed stool and soaked in the warmth and familiarity of the shabby room. The unlikely mixture of fresh straw and paint thinner was as beloved to her as new-mown grass in springtime.

She closed her eyes, cosseted in the womb-like environment—trying to regain her equilibrium. She had to think clearly now. Get her mind off of Hurricane Hunter, who was rapidly whirling her safe, orderly existence into oblivion.

Damn him anyway.

Unable to dwell any longer on her undeniable attraction to him, Quinn grabbed a quart can of bright blue paint and slapped a base coat on the Christmas soldier's cardboard helmet.

A gentle tap on the door was followed by Marla's carrot-top peeking around the frame.

"May I come in?"

"Sure. Grab a seat." Quinn lifted a bundle of old clothes and dropped them on the floor.

Marla plunked down and laid her coffee mug on the worktable. She pointed to the pile of clothing. "Cleaning closets?"

"No, stuff I picked up at yard sales. I'll cut and patch and make a wardrobe for the scarecrows."

"Oh," Marla said quietly. She looked around the workroom as if she had never seen it before. "That's a great elf."

Quinn looked at her curiously. "Marla you sat here and jabbered the entire time I built him. How come you're acting like you've never seen him. What's up?"

Marla picked up her mug and drank deeply. Setting it back down, she picked at her fingernails as if stalling for time. "I . . . uh . . . I'm a little worried about you, that's all," she finally blurted out.

Slowly replacing the lid on the can of paint, Quinn took her time answering. "Worried? About me? I can't imagine why."

"Well, for one thing you never mentioned Gabe to me and he's so wonderful I can't imagine how you forgot him."

"I see," Quinn said. Now she understood; Marla's feelings were hurt because she apparently hadn't confided in her. After all, they had been sharing secrets for over two years. Quinn unwound a length of heavy-duty aluminum foil and began to cover a cardboard sword.

"Marla, I never mentioned Gabriel Hunter because I never knew he existed before yesterday."

How odd that sounded when spoken aloud. How could anyone have gained such importance in her life in a single day?

Marla shook her bright red curls in confusion. "Quinnie, this isn't like you. At all. I mean, when you were so involved with David Simmons, it was at least six weeks before I saw his car parked out front all night. And now you've got this guy staying here on the first date? See why I'm worried?"

Quinn put a dab of hot glue on the shaft of the sword to hold the foil in place. Setting it aside to dry, she turned and patted her friend's freckled cheek. "You're priceless, you know that?" She laughed. As usual, Marla had applied her own brand of logic to the situation. She put A with B and was sure she had learned the entire alphabet. "He is not my lover, boyfriend, paramour, or any other romantic designation you've thought up in that twisted little brain of yours."

"Well, who is he then?"

"He's a . . . uh . . . ." How could she describe their unusual relationship? He wasn't exactly a friend. Not a relative or business associate. And she was forbidden to disclose their true peculiar connection. Her fine-grained brow furled in concentration. "He's . . . my houseguest!" she announced triumphantly.

"Why?"

Why, she wants to know. "He came with the cat," Quinn explained none too clearly.

Marla wasn't to be put off. "Where did the cat come from?"

Quinn stood up, wiping a smear of blue paint from the workbench. "Remember, I told you yesterday—Mrs. Featherstone."

Marla folded her arms across her ample chest. "Quinnie, I'd believe almost anything you told me, but you cannot convince me that old lady willed you her kitty and that gorgeous hunk!"

Grinning wickedly, Quinn handed Marla her mug. "In a manner of speaking, that's exactly what she did. Now, if we can have a break in the interrogation, I have to load the new scarecrows and go get the shop ready to open."

Marla left, not even partially satisfied with Quinn's explanation, muttering darkly that she would have the truth if she had to resort to peeking in windows and listening on party-lines.

Not that Quinn actually believed her friend's dire threats. She was still relieved that she'd have most of the day in the Scarecrow Emporium to think of a story that wouldn't stretch the truth too far, but would still satisfy Marla's curiosity.

After a rejuvenating shower, she pulled on an oversized turquoise shaker-knit sweater and jeans. Stuffing her pants legs into a pair of suede boots, she felt better equipped to face the day. As she brushed her hair, she felt her confidence returning with each stroke of the brush.

All she had to do was keep her main objective in mind at all times—and that was to study Gabe and see if he was the kind of person that Elvira Featherstone would have wanted to inherit her estate. Simple.

Gabe met her at the back door as she struggled with a pasteboard box of scarecrows. "Here, let me help."

Gratefully handing over the unwieldy carton, she held open the car door while he wedged it into the back seat.

Gabe straightened up and looked around, sniffing the air appreciatively. "I love that smell. Fresh air, pine needles, and wood fire, all mixed together."

"Mmm. I know what you mean. When I go down to the city, my lungs clog up in an hour."

"Yep, there are some true advantages to the country."

Quinn blinked. His words were innocent enough, but a

deeper meaning seemed to be floating just beneath the surface.

As if to confirm her suspicions, Gabe cocked his head and looked at her searchingly. "You know, Aunt Elvira was always trying to lure me up here. Now I wish I'd have given in."

Me too, Quinn thought with a jolt. Now where did that come from? The man was talking about fresh air and quiet living. Still, she couldn't help but wonder what Mrs. Featherstone might have offered as bait, when she lured her nephew.

"I'd better get going." She settled behind the steering wheel and inserted the key into the ignition. Suddenly reluctant to leave, she asked, "What'll you find to do all day—while I'm at work?"

He closed the car door and sunk down on his haunches until their eyes were level. "Oh, I'll stay busy. Anything you want me to do while you're gone—besides cat-sit?"

"No, I can't think of a thing." To escape his piercing stare, Quinn allowed her gaze to stray to the pile of uncut firewood stacked against the side of the house.

His pale gold eyes followed hers. "Okay," he groaned, "guess I have to earn my keep some way. Where do you keep the axe?"

"On the workbench in the garage, but you really don't have to . . ." she said as she slid behind the steering wheel.

Gabe brushed back a strand of ebony hair that kept falling over his forehead. "I know I don't *have* to, but I'm not much of one for Saturday morning cartoons."

She looked into his tiger eyes, impossibly gold in the early morning light. "What I meant was, that, well, you're from the city and not used to chopping firewood and . . ."

"Ho-ho, a challenge! You didn't have to resort to subterfuge, I intended to chop the wood."

She shook her head, confusion mirrored in the darkness of her eyes. "Subterfuge?"

"Sure. A not-so-subtle dare to my masculine ego."

"But I . . . that's not what I meant!"

Gabe rose and shut the car door with more force than necessary. "Go sell your scarecrows, m'lady. Your faithful serf will feed the cat, chop the firewood, make the beds, wash the dishes, toil the fields . . . don't worry 'bout me, ma'am. That cup of coffee and burned eggs will do me just fine."

With a wave of his hand, he walked back toward the house, still muttering and gesturing to some unseen audience.

Stifling a giggle, she put the car into gear and backed down the drive, passing a bright red sports car—apparently Gabe's.

What was it Marla had called him—a hunk? Poor, blind Marla. Still so immature as to be taken in by a good-looking, fast-talking man. She, on the other hand, was older. Wiser.

Oh, not that she didn't enjoy his company. She could use a little lighthearted fun. But Mr. Hunter was no one to get serious about.

But he was definitely not boring.

She had to admit that she enjoyed his ready humor. But when she got down to assessing character—she wasn't sure how much that meant. As a matter-of-fact, what criteria would she use to assess his character?

This wasn't going to be as easy as George Shaw had tried to convince her.

But it would be a lot easier, she reflected, if Gabe Hunter would keep his golden, black-fringed eyes closed when she was around.

Despite her earlier resolve, Quinn felt a quickening in her chest and her stomach did a curious somersault.

SIX

By the time Quinn opened the store at ten, funeral gray thunderclouds had settled over the village like a shroud. She glared at the dark sky, as if her scowl could forestall the approaching storm. She couldn't afford to miss the normal Saturday flow of customers. But despite her most fierce glower, within minutes the clouds opened, spilling their angry contents with a vengeance.

Wrapping her arms around herself against the chill-sharpened air, she stared out into the gloom. No one would be likely to venture up the mountain in this storm. It had been pointless to open the store.

But her mind wasn't really on the weather or the short-age of customers. No matter how she tried to force her concentration on the business, her thoughts kept traipsing back to her cabin three miles away. What was Gabe doing? Could he too be staring out into the storm, thinking of her?

A bright flush painted her pale complexion. Such fool-ishness, she chided herself.

Quinn paced the small store, looking for something to occupy her fertile imagination. There were bank accounts to reconcile, bills to pay, and supplies to order. Why couldn't she concentrate on her business?

Resolutely, Quinn sat down at the small desk behind the sales counter and pulled out a red ledger. She stared at the pages. The neatly printed entries blurred and fused with fragments of her preoccupation.

She picked up a bill for fuel. Sixty dollars. As she wrote the figure in the proper column, the sixty dollars became sixty days—the short span of time allotted in her life for Gabriel Hunter.

A twenty-four dollar invoice from the feed store for hay reminded her that twenty-four hours had already been subtracted from that scant allotment.

She slammed the ledger closed. This was ridiculous. She was mooning like a lovesick schoolgirl. Gabriel Hunter was a symptom—a reminder that she had perfectly normal physical itches that hadn't been scratched in a very long time.

Giving up on the bills, she walked back to the front of the store and stared into the darkness. As she watched, rain hit the window and rolled downward in a single sheet, reminding her again of Gabe. She closed her eyes, recalling the image of him curled in sleep, with the single bed sheet falling carelessly off his body. A heated flush spread through her stomach and she pushed the titillating image aside.

At noon, she threw up her hands. Maybe the rain would clear by the afternoon. That would still give the shop owners some chance of trade on Sunday.

She was beginning to feel the effects of going without her breakfast, so she threw on her yellow plastic slicker and darted to the restaurant around the corner for lunch.

The Copper Kettle was Quinn's favorite lunchtime haunt. Not only was the food excellent, the staff was jocular and friendly, just what she needed to dispel visions of Gabe padding barefoot down her hall, his jeans unsnapped and enticing.

For once, no crowd of hungry diners mobbed the cafe. A few locals waved a greeting, but for the most part the place was empty. She took her usual seat at the counter.

"Hey, Quinn," said Dee Anne, the intrepid lunchtime waitress, as she set a menu and a glass of water in front of her.

"Boy, your business isn't booming any better than mine is."

"Yeah, this lousy weather. Oh, well, at least we don't have to shovel it."

"Yet," they both added simultaneously.

Everyone on the hill knew that this cold icy rain could be a portent of the year's first snowstorm.

Quinn ordered a burger and cup of coffee. Dee Anne clipped the ticket on a revolving stainless steel rack and poked her pencil through her wiry gray hair. "So what's new?"

Quinn shrugged. "Nothing much."

Dee Anne's penciled brow shot skyward. "That's not what *I* hear."

"Oh?"

"*I* heard a certain unmarried resident of our fair community was seen entertaining a *very* sexy member of the opposite sex. All night."

Quinn groaned. This town didn't need a telephone system, the local grapevine was much faster—and more suggestive. "Marla had lunch already?"

"I don't know what you mean," Dee Anne lied glibly.

"Sure. Well, for your information—and so that none of our fellow citizens get blisters on their fingers from dialing their phones—my guest is a business acquaintance. Nothing else."

"Sure." The waitress nodded sagely. "I understand."

Her tone clearly implied that she didn't believe a word of Quinn's explanation.

Dee Anne turned away for a moment and returned with Quinn's burger. "Your business partner got a name?"

"See—that's how rumors start. He isn't my partner. And yes, he has a name. Could I have some ketchup, please?"

"How about dessert?" Dee Anne asked as she returned from her coffee refill rounds a few moments later.

"Mmmm. What kind of pie do you still have?"

"Take your pick," The waitress pointed to the large white board on the wall that listed the varieties of pie available.

"Too many choices," Quinn said. "Just bring something loaded with calories."

"The best kind," Dee Anne agreed and went after the pie.

She was back a few moments later with a thick slab of banana cream.

Quinn choked in surprise. With some two dozen types of pie available, how did she manage to choose this one? Good heavens, had it only been yesterday that she and Gabe had wrestled over that slice of banana cream pie? It seemed like he'd been part of her life forever.

"Okay, Quinn," Dee Anne leaned both elbows on the counter. "Fess up. Tell me all about tall, dark, and handsome."

"More like tall, dark, and irritating," she grumbled. "Really, it's no big deal. He's the nephew of an old friend of mine. He was up here on business. We had that terrible rainstorm, so I put him up for the night. Simple."

Funny, Quinn mused. She'd told the truth, yet obviously there were shades and permeations of the truth because her relationship to Gabe was much more complex than the bare bones of her explanation.

Dee Anne's smirk told Quinn she hadn't believed a word.

Quinn paid her bill and laid a tip beside her empty plate. Shrugging on her slicker, she went back out into the driving rain. Too late, she thought, she should've taken home a piece of that pie for Gabe.

But she wasn't going back and risk more questions. She had implied that he was gone now. She didn't want to have to tell an outright lie. There were some things, she noted, like privacy and anonymity, that were possible in a large city, but were luxuries in a small town.

Still, she wished she had purchased that pie for Gabe.

What was he doing now, she wondered, as she hung her dripping raincoat on a hook in the backroom. She glanced at her watch. Almost one o'clock. They had eaten an early breakfast and not much of that. Would he be fixing his lunch? Quinn closed her eyes, visualizing him putzing around her cabin, washing dishes, stoking the fire, whistling while he performed the small, mundane tasks of daily life.

A wide smile creased her face as she imagined herself a cricket on the hearth, watching him struggle with the unfamiliar chores.

Quinn decided such mundane tasks as making beds and washing dishes would be uncharted territory to Gabe. She had him all figured out. The quintessential Southern California bachelor. Happy hour at El Torito's on Friday nights, jogging on the beach, and grazing on tofu at salad bars. Yes, it was certain he didn't spend his free time on domestic chores. With his charm, he no doubt attracted an endless stream of beach bunnies anxious to take care of these minor details for him.

Quinn's brown eyes clouded as an unexpected spasm of jealousy shot through her at the specter of Gabe, surrounded by bikinied blondes. Oh, she knew the type he would go for. Tall, bosomy dropouts from a Las Vegas chorus line. Probably wore their ostrich feathers and drank white wine while they dusted. She doubted whether there was any flannel sleepwear in the lot. No wonder he found her footed pajamas so amusing. The man was hopeless.

Quinn's over-active imagination had churned up an emotional storm only equaled by the work of Mother Nature outside when the phone rang.

"Good morning, Scarecrow Emporium!" she snarled into the mouthpiece.

A hesitant silence hung on the line. She took a breath and clenched her teeth. When she spoke again, the inexplicable anger had simmered to mere annoyance. "Anyone there?"

"Hmmm, having a good day?" Gabe's facetiousness sparked over the wires.

"Not especially," she retorted, wondering why just the sound of his voice could make her cranky and bitchy.

"Uh hum," he cleared his throat, an unusual hesitation in his tone. "Well, uh . . . are you busy?"

Quinn bit her lip. She was still mad about the blondes cleaning his apartment, but she couldn't tell him that. "As a matter-of-fact, I am," she said sharply, and then amended, "sort of."

"I see."

Again there was that strange hesitation. Almost a timidity in his tone.

"Well, I won't take a minute," he said. Silence built to the count of eight. "Do you have any rags?" Gabe blurted unexpectedly.

"Rags? What kind of rags?" Her brow furrowed in confusion. The man was an absolute enigma.

"You know, the kind I can throw away when I'm done."

"Done with what?"

Again, a long silence preceded his response. "Oh, just some cleaning."

Quinn felt a slash of shame. She had been mentally convicting him of crimes while he was cleaning *her* house. Just because she had to fight her attraction to him didn't give her the right to be so unfair in her assessments of him. Elvira Featherstone had trusted her.

"Gabe, that's really sweet. But unnecessary."

"No," he said quickly, "I don't mind. Idle hands being the devil's tools and all that."

"There's a huge cardboard box in my workroom. But you really don't have to . . ."

"I know, but it's the least I can do. Your kind hospitality. Taking McLeish while I get relocated . . ." His voice trailed away.

For the first time, she noticed an undercurrent in his voice. Jittery. Nervous. Like he couldn't wait to break the connection.

"Okay," she said, "I guess I'll see you tonight."

Slowly replacing the receiver, she thought about the strange conversation. Maybe she had misjudged him.

He was a very complex man. Abrupt. Flippant. Sensitive. Witty.

She shook her head, remembering the various facets of his personality she had already seen. When she first met him in Mr. Shaw's office, he had been cold and business-like. Fast-talking, abrupt—like a child with a short attention span. But when they had been talking at lunch yesterday and by the fireplace last night, his speech had slowed and become almost laconical as if he was being relieved of pent-up tension.

The rest of the afternoon dragged by as Quinn dusted shelves and straightened stock in the storeroom. Not a single customer entered the store.

She imagined the day was dragging for Gabe as well. Cooped up in a stranger's house with only a hostile cat for company. And his hostess had been no less hostile.

Guilt washed over Quinn as she thought about her behavior since she had met Gabe, unfairly judging him by other men she had known. Just because he was good-looking—wonderful looking, actually—was no reason to label him an irresponsible playboy.

Well, she'd make it up to him. It was obvious that her fortune wasn't going to be made at the shop today anyway. She would close early and go to the market. Maybe splurge on a couple of juicy steaks and salad fixings.

Just imagine that guy, she thought warmly as she flicked

off the lights, tidying up her house, doing those small, irritating household duties which she so disliked. And she had been hesitant to even trust him to chop wood!

How foolish she had been. Obviously, Gabe had everything under control.

The front door was standing wide open when Quinn pulled up in front of the cabin.

She juggled the brown paper grocery bag onto her right hip and closed the car door with her left. "Hello, Gabe?" she called, thinking he must be around the side of the house. Probably still chopping and stacking firewood.

She stepped lightly across the front yard. The stubby heels of her shoes pocked the ground as she walked. Darn, if she wasn't careful, she'd ruin them. And new shoes were a luxury—not a necessity—on her budget. She called again. "Gabe, are you out here?"

No answer.

Quinn stepped around the corner of the cabin. The firewood was chopped and stacked neatly on a wooden pallet against the cabin.

"Gabe?"

With a shrug, she shifted the grocery bag to the other hip and minced back across the yard on her tiptoes. Maybe if she cleaned her shoes as soon as she took them off, they wouldn't be a total loss.

Climbing the steps to the front porch, she again looked at the gaping front door. Shaking her head, Quinn allowed a smile to cross her face. Somehow Gabe's absentmindedly forgetting to close the door was endearing. She could imagine him so engrossed in his chores that he simply forgot. But she was going to have to caution him about leaving it open. While crime was a relatively unknown commodity in the little mountain community of Idyllwild, California, there was no sense issuing an invitation.

She slammed the door shut behind her and lugged the

groceries into the kitchen. The room was clean and orderly, but still no sign of Gabe. Or McLeish.

Suddenly, Quinn remembered the red sports car that had been parked in the driveway when she had left that morning was no longer there. Where could he have gone in such a hurry that he left the house wide open?

Her eyes narrowed as new possibilities occurred to her. What if the cat had gotten loose? Or, worse, what if there'd been an accident?

A sick, panicky feeling swept through her body as she imagined Gabe's powerful arms lifting the axe high over his head and swinging downward with all his force. And hitting his foot.

A cold sweat broke out on Quinn's face. No!

"Gabe?" she called again, with a frightened edge to her voice.

Only the silence of the empty house responded.

Now calm down, Quinn, you're over-reacting. Gabe couldn't be seriously injured or he wouldn't have been able to drive his car.

The simple logic brought a measure of relief. Okay, so it was unlikely *he* had been injured—but what about the cat? Maybe Gabe flew out the door on his way to the vet?

With a growing feeling of trepidation, she started down the hall toward her workshop. "McLeish, are you here? C'mon on, boy. Come to Quinn."

No feline response greeted her.

Pushing open the door to the workroom, she stopped, too stunned to take another step.

Someone, McLeish apparently, had fought a mighty battle with the can of bright blue paint she had left on the workbench.

And the paint won.

The quart container lay on its side in a vivid blue puddle. The last few droplets still dripped from the lip of the can. The room was a total shambles. Her box of old clothing was scattered haphazardly. Automatically, she bent over and picked up a pair of dungarees. Like the other items strewn about, they were liberally spattered with blue paint. Ruined.

Everything was ruined.

Then, she noticed a trail of tiny blue paw-prints dancing along the beige carpet, back into the hallway.

"Oh no," she groaned, "what else has been destroyed?"

Ignoring a knot of dread in the pit of her stomach, she followed the trail down the hall. Here and there blue paw prints marred the pristine white walls. In one spot, there were discernible prints almost three-feet high—where McLeish had no doubt been jumping for joy.

"McLeish, when I get my hands on you . . . you're dead," she muttered.

The trail led into her bedroom.

Quinn stood, her mouth open with shock, and surveyed the wreckage. The laundry hamper was overturned, its contents spilled and marked with still glistening smears of blue. Beside her bed, her reading lamp lay on the floor—its dented shade a casualty of the battle.

This was it, she was definitely going to throttle that darned cat.

Then, Quinn saw the quilt.

Her most cherished possession, passed down from her grandmother, lay in a crumpled heap on the bed. Biting her lip, Quinn fingered the rose satin patchwork, now stained with royal blue.

Tears stinging her eyes, she clutched the quilt and sank onto the bed. She could have handled the carnage in the workshop, even the ruined carpeting. But she just didn't know how to cope with the loss of Gramma's quilt.

Gramma had started the quilt a few weeks after the death of Quinn's mother. In the evenings, Quinn would curl up next to the older woman on the sofa and watch as her still-nimble fingers made the tiny, perfect stitches. The fabric, the rose-colored satin, had been cut from Quinn's mother's wedding dress.

Gramma had presented her with the beautifully crafted quilt that year on her twenty-first birthday. It was the last hold Quinn had on the past. Gramma was gone now, like her mother. Pop, well, Pop was more gone than here. And now, Gramma's quilt.

A solitary tear escaped and slid down her cheek.

A movement by the doorway caught her eye. McLeish, keeping his body low to the floor, slunk into the room. His normally arrogant posture completely absent, he was the picture of abject supplication. All four paws were paint dipped, like he was wearing lilliputian blue galoshes.

"Mrrow!" he cried, jumping onto the bed.

He meowed loudly and rubbed his ginger face against her. He might be only a dumb animal, but he seemed to realize that several of his nine lives were in jeopardy.

Despite herself, Quinn felt her anger toward the cat fading. It wasn't his fault. She'd been the one who left the can with the loose lid so accessible. You couldn't blame a cat for being curious, it was their nature. And she shouldn't be so attached to . . . to things. It was just a quilt. A few scraps of old fabric stitched together to provide warmth.

But in her heart she knew it was much more than that. That quilt was her inheritance. Crafted with love and meant to be passed down through the generations.

"Mrrow!" McLeish insisted, then licked the top of her hand with his sandpaper-like tongue.

Deciding that was cat language for an apology, Quinn wiped the tears from her eyes and scratched his head. "That's okay, big guy. It wasn't your fault. I should have put that paint can out of reach." *And someone should have been watching you, knowing you'd want to explore the new surroundings. Someone who knew you were a bundle of nosey energy.*

Apparently finished with his apology, McLeish waved his tail in the air and leapt gracefully from the bed.

Wondering if there was any possibility of salvaging the quilt, she lowered her gaze to examine it. But her eyes never made it to the quilt. She was too distracted by the bright blue smear on her rose-colored silk blouse.

"Dammit!" She jumped up and ripped off the blouse. What else could happen? And why did every disaster always happen to her?

Suddenly, her bout of self-pity was pushed aside by a healthy dose of self-righteous anger.

Gabriel Hunter! He was responsible for this catastrophe. Why hadn't she listened to her own instincts? From the moment she'd first laid eyes on him, she'd recognized him for what he was—an immature, undependable, irresponsible . . . jerk!

And where was he? More to the point, where had he been while the cat had been running amok, destroying her home?

When she got her hands on that man . . . Well, he'd better look out, that was all. This totally stupid situation was never going to work. He could just pack up his cat and head back to Del Mar. *After* he cleaned up this mess.

A dark shadow fell before her.

Quinn whirled around.

Gabe leaned in the doorway, his pose relaxed, almost nonchalant.

But there was nothing relaxed about his demeanor. Tension radiated from him like sound waves, filling the room with an invisible yet powerful force. Even through her anger Quinn could see the muscles twitching in his clenched jaw, the white fury on his tanned face.

His tight expression only fed her anger. What did he have to be mad about? He should be looking humble. Ashamed.

Stalking across the room, she stopped two feet from him. "You," she pointed at his face with her forefinger, missing his nose by a scant inch. "How could you let something like this happen? You're the one who told me that cat had to be watched every minute. It must've taken him . . . hours . . . to do this much damage! Where the hell were you?"

"You're early," he gritted from between clenched teeth. "I didn't expect you for another couple of hours."

"Obviously!" Gabe said nothing. He continued to stare at her with his darkly amber eyes.

After a moment, Quinn blurted, "Don't you have anything to say to me? An explanation, maybe? Even, if it wouldn't destroy your precious ego, an apology?"

He cocked his head. A strand of dark hair fell in a comma in the middle of his forehead. With a sardonic half-grin, he murmured, "Maybe I'd find it easier to talk if you didn't look so . . . enticing."

She glanced down. With a yelp of dismay, Quinn remembered yanking off her blouse—and not replacing it. She was standing here arguing in her brassiere.

With a snarl of disgust, she stalked to her closet and pulled on her bathrobe. Wordlessly, she crossed the room and stood before him again. With all the dignity she could muster, she tossed her head. "I'm sorry if I unduly enticed you. My blouse, of course, was ruined in this fiasco."

Gabe shook his dark head. "I'm sorry, Quinn. I would have had it cleaned up before you got home, but . . ."

"Cleaned up!" she cried. "The only thing that would help this mess is to bring in a demolition crew. Tear the whole thing down. *That* would be an improvement."

The taut muscle beneath his stubbled jaw twitched. Since when did razor stubble look so good? She shook her head in self-disgust. How could her hormones be so fired up that she would think about his physical attributes at a time like this?

Suddenly, she realized he was speaking to her. "What?"

"I said I was sorry. Don't worry, I'll take care of it."

Her voice rose two octaves. "Don't worry? I'd say I have plenty to worry about. My life has been a total shambles since you walked into it. I'm not the jinx, Gabe.

You are. You're a walking, breathing disaster getting ready to happen. And I don't need any more bad luck.'' She broke off as fresh tears filled her eyes.

She gulped, trying to dislodge the lump wedged in her throat. She wouldn't cry in front of him. She wouldn't give him the satisfaction.

Gabe pushed away from the door frame and took her shoulders in his strong grasp. "I said I was sorry. I said I'd take care of all the damage. What more do you want from me?"

Quinn looked up through tear-blurred eyes. "I want you to leave. Now.''

SEVEN

Gabe tugged at his right sleeve where a little strip of white was peeking from beneath the cuff. Quinn thought irrelevantly that the chilly weather must really be bothering him—he'd donned long johns. She also thought that he was going to ignore her demand.

Finally, he looked up and captured her gaze with eyes, dark and stormy as the downpour outdoors. "All right," he said quietly. "I'll leave—if that's what you really want."

"What I want is something to go right for once. I *want* to run my little business." Her voice rose dangerously as she continued, taking all of her frustrations out on Gabe. "I *want* to bring my father out of the convalescent hospital. And I *want* you to go away."

She swiped at an errant tear leaking from her eye. "And take that . . . that feline devil with you!"

As if realizing that he was the maligned subject of their loud quarrel, McLeish jumped onto the bed. Waggling his fat rump, he yowled loudly and began scratching at the ruined quilt.

"McLeish, no!" Quinn shrieked, racing across the room. She swiped at the cat's backside. In her mind's eye, she could imagine the delicate fabric shredded by his sharp claws. "Get down. Now!"

Frightened by her tone, the cat leaped from the bed and onto the dresser in one smooth glide. The antique wobbled with the force of his landing, frightening the animal even more.

"Mrrrow!" He raced down the length of the dresser, heading for Quinn's collection of antique crystal perfume bottles.

"No!" she and Gabe chimed in unison.

Moving in concert with one another, they raced for the dresser. McLeish did a ten-point dive, landing on all fours, three feet away from the dresser.

Quinn reached out a flailing arm to grab him, lost her balance and fell into Gabe, running from the other direction. She clutched his shirt for support.

Thrown off-balance, Gabe wrapped one arm around her, and reached for the bedstead with the other. His hand slid uselessly down the length of the polished wooden poster.

Like a slow motion sequence in a film, Quinn felt herself falling. Gabe tumbled on top of her.

She cried out as a burning white pain shot through her ankle as it slammed into the corner of the dresser.

"Quinn, are you hurt?"

Gabe's anxious voice seemed to come from faraway. Her foot hurt so badly it took her breath. Gritting her teeth, she fought the tears that rose to fill her eyes.

"Quinn. Quinn. Honey, where are you hurt? Can you answer me?"

His gentle fingers stroked her face, her head. Moving down her body, gingerly probing her limbs.

With a moan, Quinn pointed downward. "It's . . . it's my ankle. I think . . . I think I broke it."

Quickly, Gabe knelt at her feet. Slowly, tenderly he applied pressure with his fingertips. "Where does it hurt? Here?"

She shook her head.

Gabe's fingers moved a few inches. "How about here?"

She gasped as he found the injured spot.

"Okay, now I'm not going to touch it again. I need to find something to immobilize your foot. Will you be okay for a minute?"

She sucked her lips and nodded.

With a light kiss on the top of her head, he hurried out of the room. The sharp edge of pain had eased somewhat, replaced by a dull throbbing keeping time with her heartbeat.

Quinn sat up carefully and rested her back against the bed frame. She could hear Gabe tearing through the medicine chest in the bathroom. True to his word, he was only gone a short time.

He returned, hands laden with magazines and bandages.

"How're we doing?" he asked softly.

"Okay. It seems a little better."

"But still hurts like hell, huh?"

She smiled weakly. Despite his faults, and they were many in her opinion, she *did* have to admit that he made a great nurse.

Keeping up a steady flow of inanities, he kept her distracted enough that she was barely aware of him immobilizing her foot.

"You know, when we were playing Twenty-Questions last night, you never told me about Quinn Rosetti." With sure fingers, he loosely wrapped a magazine around one side of her ankle, then secured it with a strip of gauze. He reached for another magazine. "How'd you happen to be up here on the mountaintop?"

"Th . . . that doesn't seem important right now," she gasped as a quiver of hot pain shot up her leg.

"It is to me," he said matter-of-factly. "For all I know, I could be up here living with a mass murderer. How do I know you don't make a practice of luring men in on rainy nights? Like those sweet old ladies in *Arsenic and Old Lace*."

"D . . . don't make me laugh. It hurts."

Looking down into the depths of her pain-wracked brown eyes, he jiggled his eyebrows and laughed fiendishly. "Ah, my pretty, I have you in my power. If you do not tell the mad Dr. Hunter *all* of your secrets, he will wrap your whole body in back issues of the *International Celebrity Tattle-Tale* and make you read them over and over." He reverted to his normal velvety voice. "So, Ms. Quinn Rosetti, how'd you end up leaving the big city lights behind?"

He cut off another piece of gauze with his pocket knife.

Quinn leaned back until she was prone on the carpet and covered her eyes with her forearm. "I was getting pretty weary of the pace myself. My parents had retired to this cabin several years before, and then when my . . . my mom died, I came home to help Pop. He never was himself after that so . . . so somehow I just stayed."

Gabe shook his head. "So, you're not hiding out from the law, huh?" He sat up on his haunches and threw up his arms. "*Voila*! Finished. Now, are you sure that you're not hurt anywhere else?"

"I . . . I don't think so." She cautiously tested her other leg, then both arms. "No, I think just my ankle."

"You didn't hit your head at all, did you?" His golden eyes were dark with concern. A startling contrast to his face which had gone pale beneath his tan.

"No. Just my foot."

"Good. Now, I want you to put your arms around my neck and hang on tight. Got it?"

"I . . . I can walk," she protested. "If I can just lean on you a little, I'm sure I can hop to the bed."

"Don't be ridiculous. You're not hopping anywhere. And you're going to the hospital—not to bed."

"No! I don't want to go to the hospital. I'm fine. Really. Just help me to the bed."

"Quinn, that's foolish. You need an X-ray."

But X-rays cost money. So did emergency room visits.

Money she didn't have to spare. But she couldn't tell him that. More than anything, she couldn't bear to have Gabriel Hunter feel sorry for her. Pity her.

"No," she insisted. "I'll be fine."

Gabe tilted her chin up with his long forefinger until their eyes were level. "This isn't up for negotiation, Quinn. You're going to have that foot X-rayed. Now, put your arms around my neck."

Quinn realized she was caught between the proverbial rock and a hard place. She couldn't stay on the floor indefinitely, and she knew her throbbing ankle would never support her weight. And Gabe Hunter's face was as resolute and immovable as a slab of granite.

"All right, I'll go. Under one condition."

"What's that?" he asked suspiciously.

"Take me to my doctor—not the hospital."

"Why?"

"Because he has all my records. Because he's closer than the hospital. Because he has X-ray equipment in his office." *And because he's willing to let me pay on credit.*

Gabe nodded his agreement. "Okay, to Dr. Johnson's office then. Now, put your arms around my neck."

Quinn followed his instructions and marveled at how effortlessly he picked her up and carried her down the hallway. When they reached the living room, McLeish was sitting on top of the television set, swishing his tail.

"Rats!" Gabe said. "I forgot about Hurricane McLeish. I'm going to have to put you on the sofa for a few minutes while I lock him in his kennel. Will you be okay?"

"Sure."

With a gentleness that belied his size, he eased her onto the sofa. Taking a couple of throw pillows, he propped her injured foot on the coffee table.

"Won't be a minute," he whispered, then raised his voice. "All right, you fire-breathing little hell cat. Let's go."

McLeish had other ideas. He'd been incarcerated in that

kennel before and wasn't relishing another lengthy prison term. When Gabe bent over to pick him up, the chubby red spitfire hissed loudly and arched his back. Every hair on his body stood at attention.

Gabe took a step back to assess the situation.

"C'mon, guy. No one's going to hurt you." He reached down again.

Whoosh! The angry animal's unsheathed claws swiped the air, barely missing Gabe's face.

"Why you little bast . . ."

"Don't call him names," Quinn snapped. "He's just a frightened, defenseless little creature."

Gabe spun around. "*He's* frightened? The little creep almost took off the end of my nose."

"Well, you're getting him upset. Be gentle with him." She couldn't stand people who were harsh with animals. This was definitely going into the report. Definitely.

Pushing back his shirt sleeves, Gabe made another charge at the defenseless creature. Again, McLeish evaded his outstretched hand and jumped gracefully onto the back of the sofa.

"Oh, for heaven's sake, let me get him," Quinn muttered. She twisted around and managed to get one hand on the frenetic mass of ginger fur.

"Mrrrow!"

"Here, sit still. Don't hurt your ankle." Gabe jumped onto the sofa behind and reached over her shoulder. "Just hang on, I've almost got him."

At that moment, McLeish did an about-face, and leaped over Quinn's head, and landed with his claws digging into Gabe's back.

"Ouch! Get this damned cat off my . . ."

"Well, hold still. You're going to sit on my . . . ow! My foot! You're hurting me!"

At that moment, the front door burst open and Marla dashed into the room. "Just what the bloody hell is going on in here? I could hear the commotion all the way across the street! What are you doing to her, you brute?"

She crossed the room in three forceful strides and grabbed Gabe's right arm.

"Damn, woman!" Gabe growled. "Let go of me."

"Marla," Quinn immediately forgot the pain in her ankle. "It's all right. Let him go."

"I will not. Do you think I didn't hear you say he was hurting you? Boy, was I wrong about this guy."

Quinn struggled to a sitting position and managed to shove Gabe's legs off of hers. Marla still had a firm grip on Gabe's wrist. His face was white and a fine sheen of perspiration shone on his forehead.

"Quinn." His voice was coldly deliberate. "If you do not tell this woman to let go right now—I will not be responsible for my actions."

Quinn reached across his chest and tugged at her friend's arm. "Marla, stop it. Now."

With a reluctant snarl, Marla released her grip but didn't let go of the subject. She backed up two paces and planted her fists firmly on her round hips. "All right, mister, I want to know what's going on."

Gabe struggled to his feet and rubbed his arm. He swiveled his dark head to encompass them both in his angry glower. "This place should be listed as a public health hazard. You should have a sign on the door—Beware those who enter here. There's no escape. Your mind and your body are in jeopardy. Turn back."

Ignoring his tirade, Quinn shifted her leg back onto the throw pillows. "Marla, I fell down in the bedroom and hurt my ankle. Gabe's going to take me to have it X-rayed."

Marla's swift gaze took in her immobilized limb. "Oh, Quinn! Are you hurt? Should I call an ambulance? What can I do?"

"Calm down, for starters. Everything's fine now."

Marla's brows dipped in suspicion. "Okay. But why was he hurting you when I came in?"

Quinn frowned. She didn't want to have to *defend* Gabriel Hunter to her friend—she was, after all, still mad at him for ignoring his responsibilities and allowing the cat to destroy her property. Still, she couldn't let Marla believe that he had been deliberately mistreating her. Recalling his gentle touch when he was wrapping her ankle, she knew Gabe wasn't capable of inflicting physical abuse. Taking a deep breath, Quinn plunged into a detailed account of the accident.

When she finished her explanation, Marla gave Gabe a sheepish grin. "Guess I made a fool of myself, huh?"

He took the few paces to Marla's side and wrapped an arm around her shoulders. "Not at all. Quinn's lucky to have a friend like you."

Marla's freckled face shone with delight.

"I have to admit one thing, though," he said. "You pack quite a wallop!"

Marla gave a hearty laugh. "Try being the only girl with four brothers. Now, I guess we'd better get this show on the road. I'll round up that feline tornado. You get Quinn to the car."

She pointed her finger right and left, like a drill sergeant organizing a complicated parade maneuver.

Gabe snapped his heels together. "Yes, ma'am!"

Marla grinned and picked up the cat carrier. "Here, kitty, kitty. Come to Marla. She has some nice tranquilizers for you."

Quinn watched her friend's adoring face as Gabe slipped his strong arms beneath Quinn's legs and lifted her to his chest. Gabriel Hunter had made another conquest.

Dr. Johnson came back into the examining room holding the exposed X-ray film in his hand. "You were lucky, Quinn. Nothing broken."

She breathed a sigh of relief. "Oh, I was so worried. This sucker really hurts."

Dr. Johnson nodded. "Unfortunately, bad sprains are

frequently more painful than actual breaks. I'll give you some medication for the pain, but no drinking or driving while you're on the medication. Got it?''

Quinn nodded. ''So, how long will I be laid up? A day or so?''

''How about a month or so?''

''What! I thought you said it wasn't broken?''

''And it isn't. But it *is* badly sprained. And I'm concerned about ligament damage. You have to give it time to heal or you can do yourself serious injury.''

Gabe interrupted from his out-of-the-way position against the far wall. ''How long does she have to be off her feet?''

Dr. Johnson scratched his chin. ''I'd like her to be off her feet for two or three days. Then crutches for a couple of weeks. After that, we can take another look at it and re-evaluate. But certainly, no standing on it for hours at your shop, Quinn, for at least a month.''

''But I can't be out of my shop for a month. In case you've forgotten, I have a business to run.''

Dr. Johnson shrugged. ''Guess you'll have to hire someone to fill in.''

''Don't worry, doctor,'' Gabe said. ''I'll see to it that she follows your orders. Oh, and send the bill to me.''

''At your address in Del Mar?'' Dr. Johnson asked.

Gabe nodded.

''No problem.''

''Don't you dare!'' Quinn tried to rise to her feet, but sank quickly back onto the examining table when a bolt of pain shot up her leg. ''I'll pay my own bills. Just put it on my account.''

The doctor looked back and forth between the two. ''I don't care who pays it, just make up your minds.''

Gabe stepped across the room and lifted Quinn from the examining table and installed her in the wheelchair Dr. Johnson had provided. ''This whole thing was my fault,'' he said, ''and I'm not going to argue about it. Send me the bill—for everything, including the medication and wheelchair rental.''

The firm tone of his deep voice told Quinn there was no point arguing about it. She was starting to realize that when Gabriel Hunter made up his mind about something, that there was no sense debating with him. She added mule-headed to his list of faults.

This was definitely going into her evaluation. Stubborn and irresponsible.

"You got it." The doctor handed Gabe a plastic vial and held open the office door.

Gabe glanced at the instructions printed on the container and stuffed it in his pocket. "I'll see that she takes these. Thank you for coming in again on a Saturday."

They made the trip back to the cabin in almost total silence. Quinn leaned back against the luxurious leather seat and thought about the ramifications of Dr. Johnson's orders. What was she going to do about the shop?

She could prop her foot up on the coffee table and work on the scarecrows in the living room. If Gabe would pull that old utility cart out of the garage she could stack all her supplies on it. That would work.

Fortunately, it was still another six weeks till Thanksgiving —the beginning of the official shopping season—although she *had* expected to sell a lot of Halloween scarecrows.

She'd have plenty of time to work on them now, but how was she going to run the shop? Maybe she could rig up some sort of stool so she could sit behind the cash register and still keep her foot elevated.

She shook her head. How would she get back and forth into town? Her car had a standard gear shift.

Maybe Marla? She always needed money.

But even as she thought it, Quinn knew it wouldn't work. As it was, Marla drove into San Diego five days a week to attend law school. She was so exhausted at night that she waited until the weekend to do most of her studying and homework.

But if Marla found out Quinn needed help, she would neglect her own studies to help her friend. Quinn vowed not to let Marla know there was even a problem.

So, where did that leave her? Maybe she should just throw in the towel and sell the Emporium. Sell the cabin, too. That would bankroll her enough so she could move to San Diego or even Los Angeles. She could always go back to work as a commercial illustrator.

She sighed in dejection. She hated living in the city. Maybe she was a hermit at heart, but this small community suited her.

As long as she could remember the family had come to Idyllwild for frequent weekends. There hadn't been many tourists then. Now, the town was invaded almost every weekend, but Quinn welcomed the tourists. They were the ones who made it possible for her to stay up here on the mountain.

Even if her father did accuse her of hiding up here, she knew she wasn't ready to give up this haven. She needed one aspect of serenity in her life. And Idyllwild was that sanctuary.

Quinn jolted back to the present when the car stopped. Compared to her VW, Gabe's car rode so smoothly she hadn't even noticed when they'd started the steep climb up her driveway.

Wordlessly, Gabe turned off the engine and pushed a button, popping open the trunk. He slid out of the car. A moment later, he opened the passenger door.

"Your carriage awaits, Cinderella." He pointed to the wheelchair.

Quinn was too dejected to even respond. Slipping her arms around his neck, she allowed him to lift her out of the car. She was surprised to see it was dark outside. She had been so wrapped up in her problems, she hadn't realized that night had fallen while they were driving.

Her head rested for a moment against his face. His

cheek, with its slightly prickly stubble, felt cool against her flushed skin. She jerked away.

He appeared not to notice her abrupt movement as he bent over and eased her into the wheelchair. She almost lost her grasp when her fingers brushed the thick, clean-smelling hair at the nape of his neck. A shiver coursed down her spine.

She was tired, she quickly assured herself. And it was getting cold outside, that was all. That's why she had shivered. A physical response to the elements—not an elemental response to him.

As if unaware of the war Quinn was fighting, Gabe pushed her up the steep driveway, along the winding sidewalk, and stopped at the base of the stairs leading up onto the front porch.

Setting the brake on the wheelchair, he reached beneath her knees and neatly scooped her up into his arms again.

A frisson of excitement blistered her skin. Her heart raced as he held her close to his chest. What in the world was the matter with her? She didn't even *like* Gabriel Hunter.

But that knowledge didn't stop her body's betrayal. Suddenly, Quinn was acutely aware of the flexing of his hard biceps as his arms strained with her weight. Then, they had reached the front door.

"Okay, Cinderella," his voice cut into her thoughts. "Think you can reach down and open the door?"

Although his tone was still light, bantering, there was a new undercurrent of sensuality in its timbre. As if by osmosis he had absorbed her physical reaction to him. Loosening one hand, she turned the knob.

It was almost a relief when Gabe finally deposited her onto the sofa. She felt limp. As if the strain of keeping her body's responses under control had drained her of energy. She slumped back against the cushions.

In the dimness of her subconscious, she heard him bring the wheelchair in from the porch. His footsteps squeaked slightly on the hardwood dining room floor, then he was in the kitchen. The muted slam of cupboard doors and the running of tap water echoed his actions.

Quinn closed her eyes. She had so much to work out, but right now she just wanted a few minutes' sleep.

"Here, take these." His voice, although soft-pitched, startled her.

"What?" She blinked, trying to assimilate her surroundings.

He waited until she was fully alert, then handed her a glass of water and two pink pills. She took the medicine and gratefully swallowed the cool liquid. She hadn't realized she was so thirsty.

Gabe lowered one hip onto the edge of the coffee table. With his forefinger, he pushed a strand of hair from her eyes. "Hungry?"

"Mmmm. Maybe a little."

"Me, too. Listen, it's late and I still have a lot to do. How 'bout if I run down to that Chinese restaurant for some take-out?"

"You don't have to do that," she protested. "There's stuff for sandwiches. And soup."

Gabe shook his head. "I'm famished. You may have the world's most glorious body—which I truly believe you do—but I'm still not used to lugging—what, about a hundred pounds?—around. I'm bushed."

She laughed despite her weariness. "My left leg weighs a hundred pounds. Gabe, I'm five-seven. And big boned. Add about twenty-five pounds to that."

He wiped his brow melodramatically. "Well, no wonder I'm exhausted. If I'd known you weighed *that* much, I'd have hired a piano mover. No, this definitely calls for Moo-Goo Gai Pan. And cashew chicken. Maybe some Mongolian beef, too."

Quinn glowered fiercely. "I'm not *that* heavy. Besides, you should be used to it. I'm sure that huge ego you lug around weighs more than that."

"Touche'." He clutched his heart. "Well, if all you're going to do is sit on your . . . petite . . . backside and sling insults at your nurse, I guess I may as well leave."

He turned away.

Quinn captured his hand and forced him to turn back around to face her. "Gabe, I'm sorry I was such a witch today."

"You weren't. Look, I'm the one who should be apologizing to . . ."

She pressed her fingertips to his incredibly soft lips, cutting off his rebuttal. Quinn shuddered as a tingle ran down her arm. Closing her eyes, she willed away the sensation. After a moment, her breath returned. "Let me finish. I over-reacted. I know that doesn't excuse my behavior, but I am sorry. And very grateful. I couldn't have managed today without you."

She reluctantly pulled her fingers from his mouth, fighting an almost overwhelming urge to press her hand to her mouth. Transfer that delicious tickle to her lips.

Gabe, as if completely unaware of the effect he was having on her, furrowed his brow in a scowl. "You wouldn't have had to manage if it wasn't for me. And you had every right to . . . to over react. Look at all the things that were destroyed—half of your scarecrows, your carpeting, wallpaper, that bedspread."

Quinn closed her eyes for a moment to deliberately banish the image of the paint-spattered quilt. Gabe felt bad enough, she couldn't add to his misery. Forcing a smile to her lips, she said brightly, "Gabe, those are only things. Things can easily be replaced. Don't worry."

"You're right, carpeting, wallpaper, all those things *can* be replaced—but they shouldn't have to be. A person's home should be their sanctuary, inviolate from destruction by other people. Or creatures! I let you down, Quinn. This whole mess is my fault. But don't worry, I'll take care of everything."

She dropped his hand and stared into his eyes, trying to fathom his meaning in their amber depths. "What do you mean?"

He leaned over and kissed her chastely on the lips. "I mean that I know you're worried about your shop. And you'll need someone to help you around here."

"No, that's not necessary. I can . . ."

He raised the flat of his hand, as if to cut off further protest. "Yes, you do. At least for a few days until you get proficient with those crutches. I don't know how, yet, but I won't leave you in a lurch. This is my responsibility and I'll take care of it."

Knowing defeat was imminent, Quinn decided to accept it gracefully. She slumped back against the cushions.

Actually, if Gabe could help her find someone to mind the shop on the weekends, Marla could carry the scarecrows to the shop for her and make the bank transactions. That might work.

With a much relieved smile, she said, "I thought you said we were going to have Chinese? How about getting a move on—I'm starving."

"Oh, God," he muttered good-naturedly, "I've created a monster. One Chinese dinner coming up."

There was a loud pounding at the front door. "Quinn, you home?"

"Make that three Chinese dinners," Gabe mumbled as Marla's red head peeked around the doorway.

"I've brought your monster back," she held the plastic kennel at arm's length.

Gabe took it from her and opened its door. The perpetrator of the day's events sauntered over to the sofa and crawled onto Quinn's lap.

"I'm off for Chinese," Gabe pointed to the leather recliner. "How about keeping Quinn company 'til I get back?"

"Sure."

He crossed the room and gently brushed Quinn's cheek with the back of his hand. "Need anything else?"

"No. Thanks." Her face burned along the path of his touch. But it was a pleasant warmth. One she didn't ever want to stop. What was happening to objectivity?

"Be right back." He winked and picked up the car keys. A moment later, the room resounded with emptiness.

Quinn sighed. Looked like she'd have to strike irresponsible from that evaluation.

EIGHT

Quinn finished the last mouthful of fried rice, and leaned back into the sofa cushions. "That was delicious. Just what the doctor ordered."

Marla, pleading a tough exam Monday morning to study for, had dished up a plate and taken it home shortly after Gabe's return.

"How's the ankle?" Gabe asked as he stood up to gather the empty white cartons.

"Pretty good. Throbs a bit when I move it."

He looked at his watch. "Time for your pain pills."

"Can't it wait a bit? They make me groggy."

"So what—you got a late date?"

He carried the empty containers into the kitchen and came back with a fresh glass of water. He stood watching until she had swallowed the medication.

"It's getting pretty late, Quinn. How about if I help you get ready for bed now?"

Her face colored. This was the part she'd been dreading. She didn't want him to help her with the intimate details of getting ready for bed, but she wasn't able to manage on her own. She should have called Marla, after all. She shook her head. "If you'll just roll the wheelchair over here, I'm sure I'll do fine."

Gabe's dark brows dipped. "There isn't enough space in the bathroom for you and the wheelchair. Let me carry you."

"Gabe, you can't carry me for the next month."

He ran a hand through his thatch of ebony hair. "I know, I know. It's just that I feel so . . . so responsible."

Sensing that he wanted to talk, she asked, "What did happen today?"

He paced across the small living room. "I finished the wood, stacked it all up. Then I did the dishes—never thought I'd get that skillet cleaned, by the way. The whole time I was working, that cat stayed under my feet."

"Maybe he was hungry?"

"That's what I thought. So I went down to the store, bought nine different kinds of cat food and new dishes. But His Highness didn't want food. He wanted me to sit and scratch his ears."

She couldn't blame the cat. The very thought of Gabe nuzzling her own ears caused her own pulse to jump a few notches. Pushing aside the vivid image, she asked, "So, what happened then?"

"Then I got this bright idea to run the vacuum. Our charge, it appears, is frightened of at least one thing in life—the sound of a vacuum cleaner."

"I see."

"Anyway, when I turned it on, he yelled like he was being chased by a pack of wild poodles and raced down the hall. So I figured good riddance to a pest and went on with my housework."

She smothered a smile at the thought of the oh-so-masculine Gabriel Hunter, swathed in a ruffled apron, wielding the vacuum cleaner.

Gabe started pacing again, his eyes lit by an internal fire while he relived his afternoon. "When I finished, I switched the cleaner off just in time to hear this crash from down the hall. I ran into your workroom just as McLeish was doing some sort of mating ritual dance in a puddle of paint.''

McLeish looked up from his spot by the fireplace. He gave them an indignant snarl and went back to licking his paws. Quinn remembered gratefully that she had used water-based paint, so at least he wouldn't harm himself cleaning the residue from his fur. Although it would serve him right to get a little ill. It didn't seem fair that he was the only one not to suffer any consequences as a result of his little adventure.

"Yeah, I'm talking about you," Gabe pointed an accusatory finger at McLeish. The cat rolled over and promptly started dozing.

Gabe shrugged and continued, "The rest, as they say, is history. While I was trying to mop up the mess, he took off down the hall again. By the time I caught up with the little bast . . . I mean pest, he had already knocked over your lamp. I yelled at him and then he jumped on your bed and had one hell of a fight with that pink blanket thing.''

Beige blanket thing—the quilt. She bit her lower lip. Gabe had no idea how important that square length of material was to her. And he'd never find out if she could help it.

One thing had become clear in his recounting of the afternoon's events—it really *wasn't* his fault. Quinn knew if she'd been home alone with the cat, the same thing might have happened.

Gabe stopped for a moment and ran his hands, fingers splayed, through his dark mane. "All of that's really no excuse. I should have locked the little demon up in his cage.''

Quinn shook her head. "We can't keep him kenneled twenty-four hours a day.''

McLeish awoke from his snooze and purred his agreement. He watched them curiously for a moment before returning to his toilette.

Quinn turned away from the cat and watched Gabe's worried pacing. He was going to wear a path in the carpet. Pausing by the window, he stared out for a moment then twisted around to face her. Taking one look at his downcast face, she felt a twinge of guilt shoot through her. She'd said some pretty awful things to him in her anger.

"Gabe, about what I said today. I apologize. I was just upset."

"And rightfully so. You were right. My first responsibility was to watch that animal. I knew what he was like —that's one mean cat!"

McLeish interrupted his evening ablutions to cast a baleful glance in their direction. He rose to his paws, now miraculously clean, and pounced onto the sofa. With a haughty wave of his tail, he dismissed Gabe and his derogatory comments, and curled up beside Quinn.

She scratched his ears absentmindedly. "He's not really mean. Just high-spirited."

Gabe snorted. "Hah! Mark my words, you'll be sorry you ever befriended the little twerp. Anyway, I'm beat. What say we get some sleep?"

After a bit more discussion on whether or not Quinn should be carried to the bathroom, a compromise was reached. Gabe helped her into the wheelchair and pushed her to the bathroom. He carried her inside the small room and parked her on the only available seat.

Then, he discreetly took his leave, saying he would lock up the house for the night while she brushed her teeth.

A while later, Quinn finished struggling into her nightgown. By hopping to the tub, she'd managed a precarious perch on the curved porcelain edge long enough to brush her teeth and wash her face. Unassisted.

"Okay, I'm ready," she called.

A moment later, the bathroom door opened and Gabe stood waiting with the wheelchair. The musky fresh aroma that surrounded him like an aura filled her senses. Her heart thudded anew as her face pressed against his chest.

Allowing her fingers to ruffle the luxuriant hair at his nape, she burrowed closer.

She was twenty-nine years old—pushing awfully close to the Big Three-O, in fact—so why was she reacting like a giddy teenager with her first crush? What was it about him that caused her heart to flutter and swoop like a kite on a windy morning in March?

Suddenly, she was aware of the fierce pounding of his heart through his shirt. His muscles rippled smoothly beneath her touch as he carefully lowered her into the wheelchair.

She felt, rather than heard, a small gasp escape his lips. Was he also caught in this electrical web? Feeling this sizzling heat? Her heart pounded faster at the thought.

But if Gabe *was* feeling more than physical exertion, he gave no outward sign as he pushed her down the hall into her bedroom.

The quilt had been discreetly removed from view. Fresh sheets were on the bed and he had somehow found the time to fill a brass vase with fragrant branches of cedar. Helping her into bed, he lifted her injured foot onto a mountain of fluffy pillows.

Gabe pulled up an easy chair beside the bed. "I'll just stay here for a while. 'Til you fall asleep."

"That's not necessary," she murmured, but didn't argue further. The pills had started taking effect and she felt the warm beginnings of sleep beckoning. "Night, Gabe. Thanks."

He took her hand and rubbed the edge of his thumb over the tender skin. "Night, babe. You get some sleep."

Sometime later, Quinn's eyes fluttered open. It was still dark. Pitch dark. The absence of light that comes only in the very early morning hours.

What had awakened her?

The room was still. Only the occasional clicking sound of the digital clock flipping over a new number broke the silence. She turned toward the bedside stand. The red numerals on the clock radio told her it was shortly after three a.m.

As her eyes grew accustomed to the blackness, she was able to make out a large shape looming beside the bed. "Gabe?"

He leaned toward her. The ambient light from the clock was trapped and reflected by his golden eyes. The expression on his face was grim. Worried. "How're you doing, babe? Ready for another pill?"

She shook her head. It hadn't been pain that had awakened her. Rather, awareness of his presence had filtered through her sleep. Without understanding how she knew, Quinn realized he had been awake all night. Watching her sleep since tucking her in.

Now that she had regained her night vision, she could see that his large frame was scrunched into the armchair. McLeish had settled in Gabe's lap and was dozing peacefully. Sometime during the night Gabe had brought the afghan from the living room sofa. It did little to cover the length of his long form. Its lacy pattern wouldn't provide much warmth in any case.

Suddenly, she felt very close to him, tied by the same mystical force that had awakened her. "Why aren't you asleep?" she whispered, not wanting to break the magical quiet.

"Just thinking." He sat up and leaned over the bed until his face was inches from hers. With a flick of his fingers, he pushed aside a tendril of auburn hair then kissed her cheek. When he spoke, his voice was unexpectedly soft, yet husky. "You missed your two o'clock pills. Want them?"

Quinn shook her head. Was it the absence of light, she wondered, that emphasized the hollows and planes of his face? Why was she suddenly acutely aware of details she'd never noticed before?

Like the way dark smudges had appeared beneath his

eyes. Gaunt hollows in his cheeks were accentuated by the room's shadowy blackness. Could she really see, or just imagine, the red rims of his eyes from the loss of sleep?

Mr. Irresponsible, she'd thought him. Why did he constantly force her to revise and upgrade her estimation of him?

She wasn't supposed to be attracted to him—she was supposed to be an impartial observer. Elvira Featherstone had counted on her to present an unbiased opinion in her report to the attorney. Quinn closed her eyes. If she didn't put a tighter rein on her galloping emotions, she was going to completely lose her objectivity.

Gabe's long finger traced the arch of her eyebrow. He had a strange, almost contemplative look on his face. "Need anything? Your nurse is on duty."

"No," she murmured. And it was true. With Gabe at her side, all her needs were being met at that moment. Then, almost of its own volition, she felt her hand raise and lightly follow the sculpted contours of his face. "You have good bone structure."

Someday, if she ever had time to pick up a brush again, she'd like to paint Gabe's face. She smiled, thinking of him sitting immobile in front of her easel, posing.

"Penny for your thoughts?" Gabe's voice rasped like finely-grained sandpaper honing marble.

Quinn snuggled deeper into her pillow. Suddenly, she was so sleepy. Her eyes drifted closed. "I was just thinking," she murmured from her half-slumber, "that someday I'd like to do you."

Gabe chuckled deeply. "I'd like that. Yes, I'd like that very much. Go back to sleep now."

With a drowsy "G'night," she turned over and drifted back to sleep.

Quinn awoke the next morning to a throbbing ankle and the enticing smell of sizzling bacon.

Only half-awake, she thought first of her father. Daniel

loved fixing a big breakfast on Sunday morning—usually something exotic and flavored with garlic and peppers. She couldn't remember the last time Daniel had been content with plain bacon.

She sat up in bed and shook her tousled hair. Raising her arms above her head, she stretched mightily. Darn, she just couldn't wake up. She felt sluggish. Groggy. Almost like she'd been . . . drugged.

Drugged. Pain pills. Gabriel Hunter.

In a flash, yesterday's full repertoire of events returned in complete clarity.

She covered her face with her hands wishing she could erase that awful day from her memory. No business at the store. The chaos when she returned home. Dr. Johnson's orders. Gabe helping her into bed.

Quinn groaned, suddenly recalling the brief moment of intimacy in the middle of the night. Had that been real—or a dream? A harmless release from the stresses of the day? Quinn hoped the latter, she wasn't ready to deal with the reality of her growing physical attraction to Gabriel Hunter.

She groaned again, louder, and turned over, punching the pillow with her fist. Why even get up? If there was one thing she *didn't* need, it was another day fraught with disaster.

There was a cheery knock and the bedroom door opened followed by Gabe poking his head through the doorway. "Good morning! And how's our patient this fine day? What's all that grumbling I heard?"

"Go away," she muttered, pulling the blanket over her head. Nothing about this day promised to be fine.

"Tsk. Tsk. Are we grumpy today?" He stalked across the room to the window. With a deft movement of his wrist, he pulled the drawstring on the heavy drapes, allowing the bright sunshine to wash into the room.

"There," he said, "isn't that better?"

"No."

A firm hand pulled the blanket from her eyes. "Rise

and shine, sunshine. Time to get that beautiful body out of the rack.''

"I don't *want* to get up. And I'll thank you to leave my body out of this." She glowered at his darkly handsome face, now as bright and expectant as a young boy's on the first day of summer vacation.

Quinn pulled her knees up to her chest and hugged them. A sharp surge of pain reminded her that yesterday had been real enough. Stretching out her leg, she watched in silent awe as Gabe zipped around the room, opening drawers, fumbling through her closet—pulling an assortment of her garments from each. Finally, he dropped the pile of clothing on the easy chair.

"Okay, Cinderella, time to face the day. Into the bathroom, brush your teeth—all that stuff. Then, instead of a glass slipper, I put a fresh wrapping on your foot and whisk you away to the kitchen where a bounteous feast awaits your pleasure."

"What bit you this morning," she snarled, "the dodo bird of happiness?"

Gabe put his hands on his trim hips and gave her a mock scowl. "Are you always this cheery in the morning? Or is this a special treat just for me?"

Suddenly ashamed of her foul mood, Quinn brushed her hair from her face and swung her legs over the side of the bed. "I'm sorry. I'm not usually such a grump, but . . .''

Without warning, her eyes filled with tears. She was mortified. Crying wasn't going to solve her problems—the past had taught her that. She almost never cried anymore, so why now? And why in front of him?

But she couldn't seem to stop her lips from quivering. Nor swallow the lump that was lodged so firmly in her throat.

Instantly, Gabe was at her side. "Hey, Quinn! It's going to be all right. Trust me."

He wrapped strong arms around her and pulled her close. "What's the matter—ankle hurt?"

"N-n-no."

"What then? Worried about your shop?"

"Y-y-yes," she blubbered. *This was so stupid. Crying wasn't going to change her predicament.* But for the first time in a very long while, Quinn was physically incapable of taking any action that would help resolve her problems.

"Quinn, listen to me." Gabe's firm hand tilted her chin, until her tear-wetted eyes met his. With the tip of his finger, he brushed away the moisture from her cheeks. "It's all under control. I told you I would take care of everything—and I am."

She pulled back and looked at him. "Wh-what do you mean?"

With a strong, gentle touch, he pushed a strand of hair from her cheek. His voice was deeper than normal and husky with unspoken emotion. "I mean that I'm going to take care of you. You don't need to worry about anything."

Quinn's heart leaped as she felt his tenderness spread over her like a protective blanket. How nice it would be to succumb to his gentle ministrations. For once in her life to lean back and rely on a man to handle things for her—instead of the other way around.

She also knew that Gabe felt responsible for her accident and she had to be careful not to exploit his sense of guilt. He could no more afford to hire someone to care for her, and her business, than she could, although it was incredibly sweet of him to offer. "Thank you, Gabe. I really appreciate the offer but I can't let you do that."

"You don't have to ask it, it's already done. I made a few phone calls this morning. Took a leave of absence from my job. Well, sort of. Actually a lot of my business is done by phone. And I have my lap-top computer in the car so I'm all set."

"I don't understand. All set for what?"

"What we've been talking about for ten minutes," he said with a hint of exasperation in his voice. "I'm going to look after you till your foot heals. Run your shop on weekends. Until you get back on your feet—no pun intended.''

"Gabe, I can't let you do that! Why you don't know the first thing about running a specialized boutique like the Scarecrow Emporium.''

His voice was suddenly strained. "I'm not an imbecile, Quinn. I have a degree in marketing. I open the doors, sell the merchandise, put the money in the register. At the end of the day, I make the bank deposit. What portion of this is too complex for me to understand?''

"I didn't mean it that way. It's just, well, what about the bills. Accounts payable. Deliveries. That kind of thing?''

He strode across the room and picked up her purse from the bureau. Stalking back toward the bed, he said, "I've already made my decision, Quinn. If there's anything I don't understand, you're only a phone call away.''

That was true. And it was also true that he would be more than capable of running the small business for a couple of weekends. After all, Marla had pinch-hit for her on more than one occasion, and Marla didn't have *any* business experience.

Gabe tossed the handbag onto the bed. "Just give me the keys. Trust me to do a simple thing like playing shopkeeper for a while.''

Here came that stubborn streak again. She'd already seen ample proof that once Gabe Hunter made up his mind, he wasn't easily deterred. Besides, she thought grimly, what choice did she really have? If she couldn't keep the shop open, she'd have to sell the cabin. And that would literally kill Daniel. During his rare times of being alert, he never failed to ask about the cabin. Quinn knew how important this small building was to her father. As long as he owned this tiny piece of real estate, he could convince himself that he was still a functioning member of society. A land owner.

No, no matter what, she had to hang onto the cabin, for Daniel's sake.

Grudgingly, Quinn gave in and fumbled for the shop keys in her purse. What, she wondered, had become of her sane, orderly life?

As she handed him the keys, suddenly the full ramifications of his intentions sunk in. If he was caring for her during the week, and working at the Emporium on weekends—that meant he would be around all the time. In her house.

His fingers closed around hers in a disquieting intimacy when he took the keys. Dropping to one knee, he leaned forward and grasped her shoulders tenderly. Pinioned in place, she lifted her eyes to meet his tawny gaze. "Trust me, Quinn, I won't let you down," he whispered then brushed her lips with his, sealing his promise.

She wanted to trust him. Wanted with all her heart to believe that this man, this incredibly wonderful man, would keep his promises.

As if he had somehow read her thoughts, Gabe said, "I need you to believe in me. After all, as of today, I'm moving in with you."

_____ NINE _____

"The first thing we have to do is go down the mountain," Gabe declared.

"Why?" She was still pondering the wisdom of allowing him to move into her house. This was no way to regain that objectivity she'd been so worried about.

"I think I'm going to need a couple changes of clothes." His cat's eyes lit up with a sly grin. "It's either that or half the time I'm going to be doing the housework in the buff while my clothes are being washed. Your choice."

"We'll go for more clothes," she quickly responded. Still, she had to admit the notion was intriguing.

He snapped his fingers in an exaggerated gesture of disappointment. "Darn! I was only trying to save wear and tear on my wardrobe."

"Sure. Nice try, buddy."

He shrugged. "Don't mind if I keep trying, do you?"

No, she didn't mind. Quinn felt the heat start to rise in her face when she realized that she didn't mind at all. In fact, despite her firm resolve to keep her emotions under control, deep in her heart she hoped Gabe *would* keep right on trying.

He reached over and laid a hand on her forehead. "Are you feeling all right? You look feverish."

Quinn bit her lower lip in frustration. If only she had inherited her father's dark complexion, instead of her mother's creamy skin. Dark-complexioned people didn't have a telltale blush on their cheeks every time their blood pressure rose a point or two.

She pushed his hand aside. "I feel fine. If we're going to the city, hadn't we better get moving?"

"Yes, ma'am. I do have one other idea."

"What's that?" She glowered suspiciously.

"Let's con Marla into cat-sitting. We don't dare leave him loose in the house and it would be cruel to keep him confined to the kennel all day."

She considered his suggestion. "Do you really think Marla deserves that?"

"Certainly. She ate most of the cashew chicken."

"You're right," Quinn agreed. "Let's ask her."

An hour later, Gabe helped Quinn settle into the front seat then wedged her wheelchair into the Porsche's small hatchback. McLeish had been delivered across the street and when they'd left, Marla was firmly explaining the house rules to the peppery creature.

The rainstorms of the past two days had faded into a distant memory. The sky was a light, clear blue dotted here and there with wispy white clouds. As they drove, the occasional scent of burning leaves added a piquant texture to the air. Indian summer. Usually only lasted a few days in the high altitude, but for now it was a magnificent time.

They decided to take a detour into town and stop at the Scarecrow Emporium so that Gabe could put a sign in the window that the shop would be closed until the following weekend. He pulled up and parked in front of the door.

"While I'm in there, I may as well take a quick look around," Gabe declared. "Familiarize myself with the operation."

"Want me to come?"

"No, you wait here. I'll just be a few moments."

With a wink, he stepped out of the bright red sports car. A movement in the window of The Copper Kettle told Quinn their activities were not going without observation.

Quinn shuddered. She wouldn't be surprised if she saw her houseguest mentioned in the next edition of the *Town Crier*, Idyllwild's weekly newspaper.

True to his word, Gabe was only inside a few moments before he emerged, carrying a stack of file folders and ledgers.

"What did you bring that stuff for?"

"I picked up ledger books and some photos I found of the various scarecrows you've made. Thought I'd go over the accounts during the week—get a head start on learning to be a shopkeeper."

"Oh." Quinn felt a sudden nibble of apprehension. She didn't want him poking into her accounts, all she wanted was a cashier until she got back on her feet. Literally.

"What's the matter?" Gabe asked anxiously. His finely drawn brows dipped, carving a tiny crease between his eyes.

A pang of guilt shot through Quinn's inflated ego. The man had offered his help. If he was a mechanic and offered to give her VW beetle a tune-up, would she turn him down? No. Gabe was a marketing consultant. She'd be a fool to spurn his offer.

Why was she acting so petty? She knew why—the Emporium had always been her baby. From idea to reality, she'd done it all herself. It was only natural she would feel a little proprietary.

Still, why turn down some expert advice? "No," she finally answered, "nothing's wrong."

Gabe's worry lines smoothed. He flicked the corners of a group of Polaroid photographs. "You know, you've really got a creative touch. These are terrific." Strapping on his seat belt, he put the car into gear and swung around, heading down the mountain. "Where'd you ever come up with the idea?"

"My Gramma's house. She was so clever. And frugal. Never wasted anything. So when clothes were worn out, she'd either cut them apart to make a quilt or put patches on them and craft a new scarecrow for her garden."

"Sounds like Aunt Elvira. She wasn't wasteful, either."

"I think it comes from them having lived through the Great Depression. Learning to make do without much of anything."

Gabe nodded. "Yeah, I guess our generation has had it pretty easy."

A broad smile creased her face. "At least that's what my father always says!"

"Yeah," Gabe chuckled, "the infamous 'when I was your age.' My dad was the same way. Walked six miles in heavy snow to get to school. The usual routine. But back to the subject. Your grandmother made scarecrows for her garden with leftover clothes. So how did you parlay that into the Scarecrow Emporium?"

Quinn leaned back in the seat and let the unseasonable sunshine warm her face. "I told you how I came back after my mother died?"

"Uh-huh."

"Well, I don't know, with one thing and another, I seemed to lack the motivation to go back to Los Angeles. But I couldn't stay here and let my father support me for the rest of my life. I didn't know what to do."

"I know what you mean," Gabe nodded, "I've been at that kind of crossroad myself."

"Anyway, one day I was going through a trunk of old clothes from Gramma's house—wondering what I was going to do with them. I couldn't bear throwing them away, some of the things had been my Gramma's when she was young. I remembered her using scraps to make her scarecrows so I thought—why not? Daniel always said there was a market for everything if it was packaged right."

"Daniel?"

"My father. I don't know, sometime after my mother died, I started calling him by his first name. When I called him Pop, it reminded me of the way he was when I was a child—he was a wonderful parent—anyway, the comparison hurt too much so I started calling him Daniel."

Gabe reached across the seat and took her hand. Quinn twitched, as if to jerk it away, then leaned back and closed her eyes. The moment was so warm, so . . . perfect . . . that she didn't want to disturb the magical spell.

"Quinn, wake up. We're here."

She felt Gabe's gently nudging hand on her shoulder. The passenger door was open and he had already brought the wheelchair around. Talk about sound sleep, Quinn thought as she rubbed her eyes. Move over, Rip Van Winkle.

She cocked her head—that might be another line of scarecrows. Characters from fairy tales and parables. Hmmm.

"You've got to get up, you've got to get up, you've got to get up in the morrr-ning!" Gabe's deep voice, singing a slightly off-key rendition of reveille, interrupted her flow of creativity.

Startled, Quinn looked up.

Gabe's broad grin creased his face in a crooked crescent. "If you think that was bad, wait till I hum you to sleep with taps."

"Hunter, you're a man of untold talents. And it's no wonder they haven't been told." Shaking her head, she took a deep breath and grasped his hand.

Bracing her with his right arm, he helped her out of the low car seat. "Boy, try your best to impress a girl and whatta ya get? Insults."

Quinn rolled her eyes. The man was irrepressible. Still, it was a pleasant change after David Simmons' constant moodiness. Artistic temperament, David had called it. What Marla used to call his personality didn't bear repeating.

Once seated in the wheelchair, Quinn looked around. They were parked in front of a small condominium unit styled in the Mexican stucco so popular in southern California. In the distance, she could hear the crash of waves and smell the pungent scent of seaweed.

"Do you mean I slept all the way to Del Mar?" she asked.

" 'Fraid so."

"Oh. Gabe, I'm sorry. That was terrible. I should have kept you company."

"You did. You have a very endearing snore."

"I do not snore."

"Are you kidding? Talk about sawing logs—I couldn't tell whether you were sawing through hard or soft wood. Although there were a couple of times I distinctly heard you saw through a knot."

"Gabe, no one has ever told me that I snore."

"Well how many people would be in a position to know?" he demanded as he locked the car door and stuffed her pocketbook into the wheelchair beside her.

"None of your business."

"Well, I'm telling you the vibration was so strong in that car that I feared for my windshield more than once."

"Gabe . . ." Her slanted eyes and raised voice warned of danger.

"Just joking!" he exclaimed, throwing his hands up in mock surrender.

Taking control of the chair, he pushed her along the inlaid red tiled walkway. It was a warm, attractive complex, she noted, very unlike the impersonal concrete and steel skyscraper that had been her home in Los Angeles. Flowering branches of purple bougainvillea draped over the wrought-iron railings. The grounds were covered with a variety of ornamental succulents amid the ice plant.

While winter was rapidly approaching in the mountains, the little seaside communities dotting the coast from San Diego to Los Angeles were still enjoying balmy weather. Del Mar was no exception.

He stopped before a ground-floor unit. A huge potted hibiscus framed the blue doorway with its peach-colored blossoms.

Gabe opened the door and pushed the wheelchair inside.

"What a lovely apartment," she breathed in surprise. She didn't know what she had expected, but it surely wasn't this perfectly-appointed room done in shades of gray and aqua. Suddenly, she was acutely aware of the image her own home presented with its mismatched furnishings and family heirlooms. There wasn't a personal item to be seen in Gabe's living room.

How cluttered and tacky her own home must have seemed in comparison.

"You like it?" Gabe asked. "I hate it."

Quinn twisted her head to follow his movements as he went to draw the vertical blinds. "You do?"

"Yeah, too cold. Impersonal."

She shook her head. "Then why, I mean, it's none of my business but . . . why don't you change it?"

He shrugged. "After my marriage to Tiffany went sour and she got the large condo I owned on the ocean, I don't know, this place never really felt like home. She'd already thrown out all of the furniture I'd accumulated before we got married so I had to start from scratch. Didn't seem worth the effort, so I hired a decorator."

Quinn was sure that she hadn't understood him properly. "Do you mean your ex-wife threw out all of your personal things, too? Photographs, and . . ."

". . . and things I'd collected on my travels. Probably not true objet d'art, but things I liked. Yep, she'd tossed them all."

A person's home should be their sanctuary. Inviolate. Words he'd uttered with intensity when McLeish had wreaked havoc in her house. Suddenly, she understood Gabriel Hunter just a little better. And liked what she was seeing.

How could his former wife have been so unfeeling?

Quinn was developing a strong aversion to Gabe's ex. She couldn't imagine if someone David, for instance had come into her home and casually discarded all of her prized possessions. Unthinkable.

Hoping to ease the pain she saw etched on his face, Quinn offered, "Maybe possessions just weren't all that important to her?"

"Right!" Gabe snorted his disgust. "Money—possessions were *very* important to Tiffany. That's why she tossed out my things, my taste wasn't as refined as it should have been. How about you, Quinn?"

His eyes looked long and searchingly into hers. "Are you a slave to the almighty dollar?"

Quinn smothered a wry laugh. "If money and fine things were my goal, I'd have to admit to being a dismal failure. No, I've never been monied and never expect to be."

"Come on," he laughed. "There's always the California lottery. I doubt that you'd turn it down if you won."

"We-ee-ll, maybe not," she admitted. "But money isn't really that important to me. As my dear father always said, 'I'd never want to be filthy rich—but maybe just a little dirty behind the ears.' "

Gabe laughed, that rich, full laugh that forced a responsive smile to Quinn's lips.

He reached over and tapped the tip of her nose with his fingertip. "You know, that's one of my favorite things about you—you always make me laugh."

Suddenly, Quinn had a glimpse into the kind of life Gabe had been living since his divorce. Lonely. Alienated from his past. Just when he'd decided he wanted to work less and share the good times with his wife, she'd decided to leave. How very hurtful that must have been. Quinn breathed a thankful sigh that she and David hadn't made it to the altar before their split.

"Want something to drink?" Gabe interrupted her ruminations.

"Some water would be nice."

"Yeah, it's about time for your pills, too."

"No. I really don't need them right now."

He cocked his head in a feigned scowl. "You sure?"

"Positive."

"Okay. Your choice. Make yourself at home while I take a quick shower and gather my gear."

Home? Quinn thought. This sterile environment couldn't be home to a monastic mouse, let alone anyone with a soul.

A few minutes later Gabe emerged from the bedroom, wrapped in a thick terry robe and rubbing his glossy black hair with a bathtowel. He wandered into the kitchen and opened the refrigerator, extracting a can of root beer. "Sure I can't get you a soda? I have diet."

"Is that a subtle hint?"

He draped the bath towel around his neck and grinned, that lopsided grin that melted Quinn's heart with increasing regularity. "Ms. Rosetti, there is nothing, I repeat, nothing, about your body that needs correcting."

Gabe leaned on the *faux* granite counter dividing the kitchen from the living room and assessed her with frank admiration. "In fact, speaking from my—shall we say, intimate?—handling of your person these last couple of days, I'd say that I think . . . curvy . . . women are a pleasure to behold. And hold."

Ignoring the shiver of delight that fluttered through her at his praise, she said lightly, "In that case, I'll take a regular cola, please."

"You got it."

He reached back in the fridge and pulled out a can. "Want ice?"

"No, it should be cold enough."

He padded across the room and popped open the can. "Here you go, one *regular* cola for a very unregular woman."

"*Un*regular?"

"What can I say? Irregular has a rather . . . well, distressing . . . connotation. And there's nothing distressing about you, Quinn." He winked broadly and chucked her chin with his knuckle. "Almost ready. Be right back."

Pulling the towel from his shoulders, he continued drying his hair as he strode back down the hall.

Quinn ran a thoughtful hand along her chin where he had touched her. Funny, she thought, the imprint of his finger still felt warm on her face.

True to his word, Gabe reemerged from the bedroom in record time.

Quinn's breath caught at the transformation. Like a chameleon, Gabe Hunter was a man of many personas. In his business suit, he'd been suave and debonair. In jeans and cotton knit T-shirts, he'd emanated a relaxed, sexy casualness. But this latest alchemy was surely the most enticing.

His hair was still damp and sculptured his head in crisp curls. A lightweight, buttercup yellow sweater accentuated the hard planes of his chest. Gray slacks curved intriguingly along his thighs, nicely hugging his tight backside.

Lucky clothing. She wouldn't mind wrapping herself around him like his clothes. The thought popped unexpectedly into Quinn's head. Now where did that come from? For heaven's sake, she was acting like she'd never seen a good-looking man before.

She released her pent-up breath as he strode across the room toward her. Actually, she acknowledged, she'd *never* seen a man who looked that good. And wasn't in love with himself.

"You okay? Need a pill?" Concern carved a frown along his smooth forehead.

"No. Why? Do I look like I need one?"

He shrugged. "You looked a little . . . spacey . . . there for a minute."

"No, I'm fine."

"In that case, you ready to roll?"

She smiled up at him, focusing on his chin as she deliberately tried to corral her raging hormones. "Aye-aye, captain. You're the driver."

"Can you carry this?"

Belatedly, Quinn noticed he was carrying a small suitcase. At her nod, he dropped it into her lap and said, "I just had a great idea. I saw a sign on the way in that they're having an arts and crafts show over at the Del Mar fairgrounds. Want to go?"

"Oh, yes!" Her head bobbed with enthusiasm. Idyllwild was an artsy community and they often had craft shows, but not, she was sure, of the quality the huge fairgrounds would attract. Maybe she'd get some ideas for the Emporium.

The Del Mar fairgrounds was only a two-minute drive from Gabe's condo.

They were greeted just inside the door by the enticing aroma of freshly-cooked hot dogs. Quinn's mouth watered. She looked up to see Gabe was apparently on the same wavelength. He was licking the corner of his mouth, his nose following the delicious scent. He looked down and caught her staring up at him.

Bowing elaborately, he asked, "Madame, she would like zee frank-furt-air, *oui?*"

Falling into his lighthearted game, she responded, "Mmmm. Madame thinks that sounds wonderful."

"Will zat be with or without onions?"

"What are you having, Pierre?" she asked, not wanting to give up onions unless he was.

"Pierre will have with. Definitely with."

"Me, too. And mustard for Madame Fifi. No relish."

"*Mai oui.* How about if Pierre parks you over here out of the way, while he fetches zee hot dogs?"

"You got it. How about over there by those wood carvings, *sil vous plais?*"

Gabe wheeled the chair over and lightly kissed the top of her head. "One hot dog or two, Madame Fifi?"

"One," she murmured, forgetting the game while trying to ignore the tingling on her scalp where his lips had pressed against her hair.

Quinn looked at all the wood carvings, and when Gabe still hadn't returned, wheeled herself around the corner to look at some stuffed dolls. She picked up a homely, freckle-faced farm girl, dressed in patched overalls. Cute. Very similar to some of her earlier scarecrows.

She turned the price tag over and gulped. How could these people get away with these prices?

Looking around for Gabe and not seeing him, she wheeled down to the next exhibit, a display of handpainted refrigerator magnets. Picking up one fashioned into an adobe hacienda, she saw that it was sculpted from bread dough. A very simple process, although the craftsman had done an admirable job.

"How much is this?" she asked when the salesclerk approached.

The girl took it from her hand and turned it over. "Eight dollars," she said.

Quinn frowned. She needed to get into the city more often. If these amounts were any indication, she needed to raise her prices again. She thanked the saleswoman and wheeled on down the aisle.

Quinn looked at the crowd of shoppers, rushing from one craft display to the other. Judging from their bulging shopping bags, she must be the only person here who was disturbed by the high prices. Was she really so out of touch with city prices? She wished Gabe would come back so she could ask his opinion.

Quinn looked over her shoulder. Still no sign of him. That must be some long line for hot dogs, she thought. She didn't want to go much farther, he might never find her in this crush.

Maybe she should go in the direction of the hot dog vendor and see if she could find him.

Turning at the next aisle, she started back to where Gabe had left her.

A few seconds later, she thought she saw him through the crowd. Quinn narrowed her eyes and concentrated on the spot where she thought she had caught a glimpse of him. There! That was Gabe, all right. Shiny hair so black it was almost blue. Dazzling white smile against his sun-darkened skin. Her heart lurched as she watched him through the mob of shoppers.

He seemed to be talking to someone. His expression was animated, his head was bent down and he was laughing with that hearty chuckle of his.

Then, the crowd shifted and she got a peek of the person he was talking to.

A tall, chic blonde. Dressed like she was going to the opening of a Broadway play. Suddenly, Quinn was uncomfortably aware of her own Levis and bulky sweater. She *had* put on a touch of makeup for a change, but still, there was no comparison between her and the perfectly groomed woman who apparently had Gabe's complete attention.

Then, she saw Gabe reach into his pocket and hand the woman something. His business card no doubt. Quinn looked away, not wanting to see anymore. Not wanting to admit how much it hurt to have him so attentive to another woman.

She glanced back up. Gabe was waving cheerfully to the blonde and loping back toward Quinn.

With a quick movement of her wrist, she wheeled the chair around, nearly hitting a young woman who had her arms filled with purchases and was towing an unwilling little boy behind her.

"Sorry," Quinn murmured as she inexpertly spun out of the woman's way.

"Hmmph!" the woman sniffed as she sidestepped the wheelchair, muttering about how thoughtless it was to bring those things into a crowded place.

Ignoring the woman's rudeness, Quinn looked up and saw Gabe was rushing in her direction. She got very busy examining a table full of crocheted tablecloths.

"There you are! I was looking all over for you," Gabe exclaimed.

Sure. Did you think that blonde had me hidden in her wallet? She said nothing.

"Here's your hot dog, madame." He bowed and presented her with the foil-wrapped treat. A cheap paper napkin was folded over his arm in a parody of a waiter's cloth. "Everyone in zee city was waiting in line." He pushed Quinn to a group of tables set aside for diners. Hitching a chair leg with his foot, he sat down across a small card table from her.

As if sensing that Quinn was no longer in the mood, he dropped the French maitre'd routine. "Hope these didn't get cold while I was looking for you. Did you see anything you wanted?"

No, did you?

Gabe frowned and looked into her eyes. "Are you all right?"

"Of course. Why wouldn't I be?"

"No reason. Thought the foot might be bothering you."

"No. I'm fine." She bit into the hot dog. It was as bland and tasteless as foam rubber. *French cuisine—phooey.*

Gabe, however, was gulping his down with gusto. "Mmmm. Delicious. Haven't had one of these since, I don't know when."

"Don't talk while you're chewing."

"Yes, mama. You sure you're okay?"

"I *told* you I was. Do I have to repeat myself?"

He laid the remains of his frankfurter on a napkin and leaned back in the chair. "Okay. What gives?"

"I don't know what you mean."

"Please, Quinn, don't play that game."

"What game?"

"That one that says, 'I'm mad about something and if you don't know what it is, I'm not going to tell you.' That game."

"I am not mad. Believe me, I'll tell you when I am."

And she certainly had no right to be, she admitted. Up until a couple of days ago, Gabe Hunter hadn't even known she existed. He'd had a life before she came along, how could she presume he wouldn't want to continue a private life that didn't include her?

"Suit yourself," Gabe shrugged and picked up his half-finished hot dog. "Oh, by the way. I ran into an old friend. She's a buyer for a department store chain in the L.A. area."

"Oh?" Quinn felt a surge of hope. Had she jumped to the wrong conclusions?

"Yeah. Madelyne Parker. I thought she might be a possible outlet for your scarecrows."

"You did?" She bit into her frankfurter. Suddenly it tasted better.

Gabe licked a smear of mustard from his mouth. "Mmm-hmm. Anyway, she said she'd think about it and give me a call."

Yeah, Quinn thought, *she's going to call you all right, but it won't be to buy scarecrows.*

Gabe finished his meal and started gathering the paper wrappings. "Used to play racketball with Marty Parker, her husband, when I lived in La Jolla."

Instantly, Quinn's hot dog tasted wonderful. *Cordon bleu*, in fact.

Gabe tossed their trash into the receptacle and they started down the crowded aisles. He smiled knowingly when Quinn showed him the eight-dollar magnets.

"I'm telling you," he said, "people will pay a fortune for things for their home. Especially if they think it's unique."

Quinn wondered again about the prices she was charging at her own shop. But business wasn't all that great with her prices the rate they were—maybe she'd best not tempt fate.

They spent a fun two hours, laughing over all the crazy trinkets. At one exhibit, Gabe bought her a stuffed monkey on a stick that danced and clapped its hands when you pulled a string.

"You remembered!" she cried, grasping the cuddly imp to her chest.

"Well, I figured it was my fault that McLeish destroyed Oscar, so please accept this as a humble token of my abject apologies."

"You couldn't pry it away from me! What shall we name him?"

"That is your problem," Gabe said. "I've never named a monkey in my life and I figure thirty-six is too old to start."

"Hmmph. Be a kill-joy. I'll think of a good name, won't I, fellow?"

Quinn couldn't remember the last time she'd had such a carefree day—nor a day when she'd laughed so much. Gabe was right, she thought. She was too serious too much of the time. She needed to lighten up.

Later, in a mood of total pig-out, they shared a fluffy cone of cotton candy.

"Mmmm," Quinn licked the sweet globules of sugar from her lips. "This has been a great day. Thanks for bringing me."

Gabe stuck a finger in his mouth, and sucked off the sticky residue. "Sure has. Just one down note, though."

"What's that?"

"Sure was sorry to hear Madelyne and Marty Parker got a divorce."

TEN

"It's still early," Gabe said when they were settled back in his car. "May as well make a day of it. What would you like to do now?"

I'd like to kick you in the shins, for starters. Instead, she smiled sweetly. "Oh, I don't know. Whatever you want." Quinn had no intention of letting him see that his comment about Madelyne Parker's marital status had hit her like a five-pound sledgehammer.

Gabe pulled out onto Interstate Five, heading north. "Didn't you say your father lives near here?"

"Not really. He's in a convalescent home in Escondido."

"That's just a short hop if we cut across."

Quinn shook her head. "I . . . I don't know if that's such a good idea."

Gabe cocked his head. "Why not? Which one of us are you ashamed of—him or me?"

"Don't be ridiculous! My father's condition is certainly nothing to be ashamed of and as for you, well . . ." *Ashamed? Gabriel Hunter was the kind of man she'd be proud to be seen with anywhere—anytime. Except, of course, when he was being a jerk. Like now.*

"Okay, then, Escondido it is." Flipping on his turn

139

signal, he maneuvered through the heavy traffic to the right lane.

"Gabe, visiting my father in a rest home can't be very enjoyable for you."

He slanted a thoughtful look at her. "Do you think I'm a total hedonist—that pleasure is my sole motivation?"

"Well, no. Of course not." Though she wondered for a moment what *did* motivate this enigmatic man.

"Look, Quinn, I want to get to know you. All of you. I'm an adult. I know people have problems, things that aren't so pleasant. Hell, so do I. But those problems are what make you—you. Now, when we get there, you go in first. If it looks like your father shouldn't have strange visitors today, then I'll wait outside. Deal?"

Well, that sounded reasonable. "Okay," she said, "deal."

The rest of the ride they engaged in meaningless chit-chat. Subjects people tend to explore when they are first getting to know one another. Movies. Theater. Sports. Only occasionally did Quinn's mind flick back to Madelyne Parker.

But Gabe didn't mention the woman again, so eventually, Quinn also forgot about their disturbing meeting.

When they reached the Shady Rest, Gabe sat in the lobby charming Nurse Kingwalton while Quinn went in search of her father.

"I think he's out on the patio enjoying the sun," Mrs. Kingwalton called as Quinn eased the wheelchair through the swinging door that separated the lobby from the patients' residential area.

Sure enough, Daniel Rosetti was leaning back in a twine hammock, basking in the sunshine, when Quinn rolled across the patio. The wheels were almost silent on the terra cotta tile and a gentle smile tugged at her lips as she stole up beside him. Pulling aside his old straw hat, she kissed him on the forehead then ducked back.

"Monkey see. Monkey do," she chanted, replaying the childhood game that had won her her nickname.

Daniel Rosetti sat up and grinned. "Well, you just wait till these ole' bones wake up—then we'll see who's the monkey!"

He held his arms out and Quinn leaned inside their loving embrace. *Another good day. Pop's new medication must be working.* It was the first time in months she'd felt anything like hope for her father's eventual recovery.

Daniel's grasp suddenly tightened. He pushed away and looked pointedly at her wheelchair. "Quinn, what happened? Did you have an accident?"

"Only a minor one. Not in the car or anything like that. Minor," she repeated.

Daniel's skeptical glare told her he wasn't going to accept a partial explanation so she gave him a somewhat edited version of her accident.

Her father scratched his chin. "Kind of skimming over why that fella was in your bedroom in the first place, aren't you?"

"Pop!"

"Just askin'. So this fella, Hunter, was it?"

"Gabe Hunter."

"Whatever. He the one you were fretting about the other day?"

"I wouldn't exactly call it fretting, Pop."

"Uh-huh. And he's the one who caused you to smash your foot?"

Quinn leaned back in her seat and glared at her parent. "It was an accident, he didn't cause it on purpose, you know. And my foot isn't smashed, it's only sprained. I told you that."

"Well, if I ever get the chance to have a few words with Mr. Hunter, I'm going to give him a little advice on how to treat a lady, that's for sure."

Crossing her arms, Quinn narrowed her eyes. Even after all these years, it was sometimes hard to tell when her father was teasing. "Too bad you feel that way," she said. "I was going to bring him in to meet you."

"Now? He's here?"

Quinn nodded.

Daniel also leaned back and folded his arms across his chest. "I'd welcome the opportunity."

She shook her head. "Not if you aren't going to be nice."

Daniel was silent to a count of five. "All right," he groused, "I'll withhold judgment until I meet him. But I'm not going to like him."

Her mouth curved down in a half-grimace. This whole thing had been a bad idea from the start, she'd tried to tell Gabe. But he wouldn't listen. Oh, well, it was his choice. Aloud she said, "But you promise you won't insult him?"

"Insult him? Why, has he got a beer gut or a hairy wart on his nose?"

Quinn shook her finger in mock consternation. "Now, don't you go embarrassing me with your foolishness, you hear?"

Daniel made a criscross motion over his chest and gave his grudging promise. "Cross my heart."

He leaned back, raising his face to the sun while his only child wheeled back across the patio.

With a lighthearted smile brightening her face, she ran her hands along the rubber wheels. This was amazing, her dad alert and feisty two visits in a row. That first thin inkling of hope grew in her chest. Maybe he was going to come out of whatever hell his mind had been locked in since her mother's death.

In a matter of moments, she was back in the lobby where Gabe was skimming through a magazine on fitness for seniors. Quinn was so exhilarated at finding Daniel lucid again, that without conscious thought, she grabbed Gabe's hand.

With a cryptic smile, he wrapped his fingers around hers. Then, releasing her grasp, he stepped behind her and pushed her back out to the patio.

"Happy to meet you, sir." Gabe took the older man's proffered hand.

"Likewise." Daniel Rosetti's frown indicated otherwise. His eyes, black as beetles at midnight, scrutinized Gabe from head to toe. Apparently, Gabe passed the first test because Daniel nodded and said, "Let's mosey over there where they've got enough chairs so's we can all sit down."

Quinn listened to the two men sparring as she navigated the wheelchair behind them. Until an hour ago, she'd never had a thought about them meeting; now, inexplicably, it was very important to her that they like one another.

And, in fact, they seemed to hit it off well. After satisfying himself that Gabe hadn't deliberately tripped her, nor had she fallen while trying to escape his evil clutches, Daniel relaxed and started grilling Gabe about his business.

Quinn smothered a grin as Gabe parried another of Daniel's probing thrusts into the younger man's financial wherewithal.

Gabe turned his head toward Quinn and winked. He knew that the older man was checking his prospects, in the manner of all Italian elders, and submitted to Daniel's prying with a good-natured smile.

After a while, Daniel's questions became less insistent. Gabe posed a couple of skillful questions of his own, and Daniel was off and running, regaling them with stories of his own business ventures.

Within ten minutes, Gabe had him laughing.

Watching Gabe melt her father's defenses, Quinn felt a tender glow of pride. Gabe Hunter was a man anyone could like. Daniel had never cared for David Simmons and spared no feelings in making his opinion known. But within half an hour, he was slapping Gabe on the shoulder and calling him son.

"Well, Monkey," Daniel said, after the two men had exhausted the subject of the current political scandal, "looks like you finally found a fella with some horse sense."

"That's only because he agreed with you on every single issue," Quinn shot Gabe an accusatory glare.

"That's not true," Gabe protested, golden eyes wide with ersatz innocence.

"Is so. Trying to butter up my father. You ought to be ashamed."

"Hell, no!" Daniel cut in. "Man should be congratulated. You think I didn't butter up your grandfather when your mother and I were courting? It's part of the mating ritual."

"Daniel . . ." she gritted.

Gabe, as if sensing an impending thunderstorm between the Rosettis, interjected, "There is one thing I'd like to know, sir," he leaned over and addressed Daniel in a confidential tone.

"What's that, son?"

"How'd Quinn get that nickname—Monkey?"

Quinn sat her tea glass on the table. "*I'll* tell you. It comes from a game we played when I was a child, Monkey See—Monkey Do."

Daniel chuckled. "Used to play that game, all right. But that's not where the nickname came from."

"Oh?" Gabe raised one dark brow and looked suspiciously at Quinn.

Leaning forward, Daniel slapped his bony knee and whispered conspiratorially. "She got that nickname 'cause sometimes she's just like a little monkey. All thin arms and legs. Never sits still for a minute. And chattering a hundred miles an hour."

Gabe burst into gales of laughter. "You . . . you're right, sir," he choked, "that *is* an apt description of her."

Brown eyes flashing murderously, Quinn snapped, "Didn't anyone tell you it was rude to refer to a person as her when they're right next to you?"

Gabe ignored her rebuke and continued to laugh, muttering Monkey over and over.

"It wasn't that funny," she grumbled. "Anyway, isn't it time we were heading back?"

Gabe looked at his watch. "Yeah, I guess so." He

sounded regretful, as though he really were enjoying their visit.

Quinn was warmed by the fact that he honestly seemed to like her father. A lot of people, she knew, judged Daniel only by his back-woodsy way of talking. But Quinn knew, and Gabe seemed to understand as well, that Daniel Rosetti had left his country roots way behind. When he wasn't lost in the dim, shadowy world that often claimed him, her father was as astute as any intellectual guru. More astute than many, in her opinion.

Gabe rose to his feet and he and Quinn made their farewells to Daniel.

"Quinnie, think you've got a winner this time," Daniel whispered in her ear as he kissed her good-bye.

A winner, huh? She hadn't even been aware that she'd entered a contest. But suddenly, she knew Daniel was right. In the narrow world of eligible men, Gabe was a blue-ribbon winner.

When they reached the car, Gabe kneeled down beside the wheelchair. Cupping her chin with his fingertips, he looked into her warm brown eyes. "Thanks for letting me meet your dad. He's quite a guy."

"No," Quinn said, "I'm the one who should thank you. Pop doesn't get many visitors, and you really brightened his day. He liked you."

"I liked him. But then, I expected to."

She twisted her head, trying to discern the meaning hidden in his shadowed eyes. "What do you mean?"

Gabe shrugged, then treated her to his crooked smile. "I mean, I knew I'd like Daniel because I already liked his daughter. Very much."

He lowered his head, slowly, deliberately. Capturing her lips with his, he pressed more insistently.

Quinn raised her head to more fully meet his. Her heart—her mind—her entire body pounded with a primal drumbeat that echoed through her to the very pavement. The outside world suddenly ceased to exist.

Time was captured and bottled in the kiss they shared.

His teeth nibbled at her lower lip, teasing. Taunting. Then his lips moved to the corners of her mouth. With the softest of pressure, he licked the sensitive edges of her mouth, then forced her lips opened as his tongue began an exploration as old as time.

Quinn accepted his probing and followed with her own tentative quest, then gained more confidence as the sound of his labored breathing echoed her own. Her heart soared as she realized this was her destiny. This moment with Gabriel Hunter was why she'd been born.

Then, as slowly as it began, their lips pulled apart. Quinn felt as if some element vital to her existence—like oxygen—had been taken away.

She wanted more.

She needed more.

And from the hungry look in Gabe's eyes, she knew his need was as great. Still, he drew further away. "Well," he said in a husky voice, then cleared his throat. "Hello, Ms. Rosetti."

"Hello, Mr. Hunter," she breathed in return, content for the moment to drink in his very essence.

Gabe ran the back of his hand from her mouth, along her cheek in a gentle trail to her cloud of auburn hair. "Right now, at this moment, you are the most beautiful creature I've ever seen."

She captured his hand, and brought his palm to her lips. "I know I feel beautiful inside," she whispered.

They both knew what they'd just shared hadn't been a kiss of hesitation, but of promises offered—and accepted.

"Penny for your thoughts."

Quinn jumped as Gabe's deep voice penetrated her mental fog. She sat up and looked around anxiously. She'd been so lost in her own private world, she hadn't noticed the miles speed by. "Where are we?"

Gabe's melodious chuckle filled the small car. "I only

hope it's thoughts of me that have kept you so preoccupied. We're about five miles from the Idyllwild cut-off.''

"You're kidding!" Quinn exclaimed. The last time she'd noticed, they'd just passed the Temecula exit. She must've been drifting for over an hour.

"I'm sorry, Gabe. I've been frightful company. I must've dozed off.''

He shook his head.

Even in the dim light of the car's interior, his teeth gleamed with what Quinn privately thought of as his demonic grin. Her mind's eye visualized the tiny laugh crinkles around his eyes, the way his lower lip thrust to the side, slightly skewing his smile.

"No sale, Quinn. You've been wide awake, staring out the window almost since we left the convalescent home. Care to let me in on it?"

She leaned back against the headrest and concentrated on the drone of the Porche's powerful engine. What *had* she been thinking?

Since Gabe had kissed her in the parking lot, her mind had been a maelstrom of conflicting emotions. Giddy. Confusing. Melancholic. Even frightening emotions.

Gabe had rushed into her life a mere two days ago, yet, in some ways, she felt she had known him since the beginning of time. He had made such an immediate impact, she couldn't remember what her life had been like before Gabriel Hunter and it took her breath away to imagine a future without him.

Yet, in the deepest recesses of her heart, Quinn knew that was the future waiting for her.

She could pretend all she wanted—as she'd been doing for the past hour. Pretending that Gabe would fill the void that had been aching in her heart for so very long, Quinn imagined more kisses, more laughter, his hands caressing her.

When she gave free reign to her errant thoughts, she fantasized them making a life together.

Gabe was funny, thoughtful, enticingly handsome, and incredibly sexy. He was fun to be with, easy to talk to. And, she acknowledged ruefully, his kiss had started a wildfire that threatened to consume her.

Even Daniel liked him and her father never liked any man who had an interest in his daughter.

Yes, if Quinn pretended hard enough, Gabriel Hunter looked like the perfect man.

But she wasn't the perfect woman for him.

She had made a pact with the devil—in the person of George Shaw, a pact that would turn Gabe's warm smile into a frosty grimace. Just before he walked out the door and out of her life.

Leaning her head against the window, she chewed on a knuckle. If only there was a way out of this madness. Maybe she could call the attorney and withdraw—plead conflict of interest or something. Maybe if she told them she had some dread disease and had to go to . . . Butte, Montana . . . or somewhere like that, for a long rest?

"Not going to answer, huh?" Gabe asked, as he expertly maneuvered the Porsche around one of the hairpin curves wrapping around the mountain.

"I was thinking . . . I was thinking how I'd love a big bowl of hot, buttered popcorn," she blurted in hasty prevarication.

"Popcorn!"

She winced in chagrin. Lying, even about her thoughts, didn't come easily, but surely she could've done better than that.

Still, she'd told that stupid whopper, so there was nothing to do but plunge on. "I can't help it if I'm hungry, can I? All you've fed me today is one lousy hot dog."

"That hot dog was not lousy! Although I have to admit I'm a little hungry, too. But, Ms. Rosetti, you can fool some of the people some of the time, et cetera, et cetera. But I know, and you know, and you know that I know, that you *weren't* thinking about popcorn for the past hour."

Ignoring the slight censure in his tone, she tried to lighten the serious tack their conversation was taking. "I don't know what you *think* you know, that I know you're thinking that I know."

"Don't try to change the subject."

"I'm not even sure what the subject is," she protested.

Gabe slammed the flat of his hand on the steering wheel. "Dammit, Quinn! Why do you always do that? Every time I try to scale that steel wall you've constructed between Quinn Rosetti and the world—you push me away and retreat into someplace I can't go."

Startled by his sudden vehemence, and by the accuracy of his accusation, she retorted defensively, "I didn't know that I did."

Of course, Quinn admitted, he *was* right about that barrier. After all, hadn't she spent the last few years perfecting that fortification? He was wrong about one thing, though, she thought with a wry grin, that wall couldn't be made of steel—Gabe Hunter could see right through it.

When he spoke, his voice was calmer although tinged with a peculiar quality that sounded almost like pain. "That's not true, Quinn. You know when you're keeping me out. What I don't understand is why."

Why, indeed? Because if she allowed him inside, if she allowed herself to care, someday he'd learn the truth and she couldn't bear the consequences. She couldn't bear to lose him.

Fortunately, the Porsche turned into the driveway and Quinn breathed in relief. For now, she had been rescued from the uncomfortable subject. But if she knew Gabriel Hunter, he wouldn't let the subject lie fallow for long.

Gabe slid out of the driver's seat and walked around to the passenger side. "C'mon." He reached across her to release the seat belt, almost drowning her in his fresh, masculine scent.

He slipped his arms beneath her and easily lifted her from the car. "Find your key. I'll carry you inside and come back later for the suitcase and wheelchair."

"All right," she murmured, laying her head in the hollow formed by his neck and shoulder.

Inside the cabin, he sat her on the sofa and knelt before the fireplace. She watched the broad expanse of his shoulders, muscles rippling beneath his cotton shirt, as he easily hefted the large logs. His well-formed thighs, accentuated by the taut material of his trousers as he hunkered down, sent a tiny shiver of desire raced through her, settling in a tingling warmth low in her body.

At that moment, she wanted Gabe as she had never wanted any man before.

Gabe seemed unaware of the effect he was having as he continued wadding newspaper and fiddling with kindling. But when he swiveled on his heel and turned to speak, there was a bright intensity in his eyes that belied the quiet, almost tender, tone of his voice. "Quinn, I'm sorry about what I said. I had no right to push you."

The fire caught and he rose, dusting soot from his hands. Never taking his eyes from her face, he silently crossed the room and dropped onto the sofa beside her. Taking Quinn's hands in his, he forced her to meet his piercing gaze.

"Quinn, when you get to know me better, you'll find that impatience is one of my less-endearing qualities. I know we've only known each other a few days . . . but . . . so much has happened. Somehow time has been compressed, throwing us together so that . . . well, dammit, Quinn, I feel like we've known each other forever!"

Quinn held her breath. So unexpected was Gabe's declaration that she was afraid to release her pent-up breath for fear she'd shatter the fragile spell his words evoked.

He draped an arm around her shoulder, drawing her close. His expressive eyes, framed with thick black lashes, looked long and searchingly into her face. "I won't rush you, Quinn. I'll try to restrain my impatience. Just give me your promise that you won't push me away. Shut yourself off."

"I . . . I'll try," she murmured, her insides quivering with his nearness.

Gabe bent forward, tilting her face up with his fingertip, until their breath mingled, his mouth capturing hers.

Quinn trembled and leaned into him. Acting on their own initiative, her arms slid around his neck and her lips eagerly sought the exquisite softness of his.

She had to be crazy. She couldn't allow this to happen. There was no future with Gabriel Hunter. But she couldn't stop her traitorous body from arching against his. Couldn't stop her heart from pounding in her chest. Nor stop the raging heat flowing through her veins.

Her fingers found and delighted in the feathery softness of his hair. It fell, thick and lustrous, through her splayed fingers as she urged his kisses to a deeper passion.

Her actions triggered a ragged gasp from Gabe. His mouth pulled away from hers, his lips raining kisses on her neck, down the smooth column of her throat. Finding and adoring the delicate satin of her ears. He dragged his fingers through her abundant auburn hair, and murmured, his voice thick with pleasure, "Oh, Quinn, darling. Do you know what you do to me?"

Quinn couldn't speak. Her voice was caught in an elegant suspension of time, anticipating the moment his mouth would reclaim hers. She twisted her head, feeling the faint rasp of razor-stubble against her cheek. Yes, she knew what she was doing to Gabe because she was aflame with a responsive fire of her own.

She closed her eyes, pushing aside coherent thought. Relishing, savoring the sweetness of his mouth. Her entire body ached with desire. She wanted his hands on her face. Her breasts. Her thighs. All of her. Every nerve ending in her body quivered with the need of Gabe's special attention.

As if in reply to her silent plea, his hands sought the loose edge of her blouse top. Sliding up the tender flesh of her abdomen, seeking and finding the sensitive fullness of her breasts.

Unexpected emotions shuddered through her, blinding her to reason, filling her with need. An overwhelming need for Gabe to assuage the emptiness inside her.

"Forget the world, Quinn," his voice whispered in her ear. "Let me make love to you."

There was nothing she wanted more than to lose herself for a few hours in the delicious strength of Gabe's arms. But this was too much—too fast. She needed time to think. To sort out the mess she'd created.

She couldn't risk loving and losing Gabe. Better not to have loved him at all. Even as his butterfly caresses tortured her fevered flesh, she stiffened in his arms.

Gabe, sensing her withdrawal, pulled back. His eyes searched hers, looking for whatever emotion was hidden in their dark depths. "What is it, Quinn? Did I do something wrong?"

She ran a trembling hand through her mussed hair. "No, Gabe. Nothing. I just need time, that's all. This is too sudden."

"Is there . . . is there someone else? Someone you haven't told me about?"

"No, of course not."

"Then I don't understand. Don't lie to me, Quinn. You want me as much as I want you."

"Maybe more," she murmured.

"Then for God's sake, why?"

His forehead furrowed in a deep scowl. She knew he was trying to understand, to make sense of her actions.

When she said nothing, he tried again. "Are you afraid I'll think less of you in the morning?"

She shook her head, afraid to meet his fierce gaze. If only it were that simple.

"Quinn, sweetheart, we've got something very special . . . dammit, this sounds dumb, but . . . but I feel almost a magical pull when we're together. Don't you feel it?"

She nodded, not trusting her voice.

"Then why won't you tell me whatever it is you're hiding? Are you afraid because you've been hurt before? Hell, we've all been hurt; you have to learn from it. Go on. But we have to be honest with each other. Talk this out.'' His finger poked her chest. "Here. Inside. What are you feeling? What are you hiding, Quinn?"

"I'm not ready—"

Pressing his fingertips against her lips, he cut off her anguished protestation. "All right, my darling. If it's time you need, it's time I'll give you. But, Quinn, I'm just a man— not a plaster saint. Being this close to you and not touching you is absolute hell. So, I'll give you whatever time you need, but, please . . . darling, promise me it won't be too long?"

For an answer, she wrapped her arms around his neck and pressed her kiss-swollen lips to his.

A sudden rattle at the front door warned them of impending interruption. Before they had time to pull apart, Marla's carrot-red head popped around the doorframe.

"Hey, guys, did you forget to pick up this hairy, monster-child of yours? Oops. I interrupted something, didn't I?"

Gabe slanted a mock glare at the intruder and turned back to Quinn. "We're going to have to start locking that door."

Quinn smiled, relieved that Gabe seemed to have recovered his equilibrium. At least, she thought with faint misgivings, he *sounded* like the old Gabe.

"Come on in, Marla," she called, then winked at Gabe. "You're right, we're going to have to lock that door. There's just no telling who the cat's going to drag in."

ELEVEN

As the days quietly passed, Quinn realized Gabe was a man of his word. Since the night they'd come home after visiting Daniel, Gabe had made no demands for further intimacy. He'd been so impersonal, in fact, that she sometimes wondered whether she had imagined the whole scene. Had she conjured it, confusing fantasy with reality?

A tiny tremor raced through her, setting her very flesh aquiver, as she relived their brief interlude. No, that had been no fantasy. Their romantic tryst had been real. Tangible. Despite Gabe's efforts to return to their earlier casual friendship, That Night stood between them. When he entered the room, the atmosphere came alive. Crackled. Like an approaching storm, ominously silent, charging the air with an electric current that amplified and overwhelmed the senses.

Where would this ever lead? Their relationship was a dead-end road. A sure path to emotional destruction. Still, she knew deep in her heart they could never regain the simple companionship of the past. Be buddies.

Besides, Quinn knew she didn't want to be his pal. She wanted to be . . . hell, she didn't know what she wanted!

For the thousandth time, she thought back to that fateful

day—and night. How had they made that swift transition from friends to potential lovers? What had triggered the intense explosion of Gabe's passion?

His running into Madelyne Parker at the fairgrounds?

Quinn could still taste the burst of jealousy she'd felt that day at the Del Mar fairgrounds. So, Gabe had run into an old friend. Big deal. A beautiful, divorced old friend. Still no big deal.

At least, not unless she made it one.

No, she didn't intend to have Gabe think she was one of those clinging, clutching women that smothered their men. Besides, he hadn't mentioned the woman again.

Quinn sat in front of the picture window, waiting for the now familiar red sports car to pull into the drive, but when the front door opened, it was Marla's freckled face who appeared.

"Hey, Quinnie. How goes the life of a hermit?"

Quinn waved her in and pointed to a chair.

Marla sank into "Gabe's" recliner. "Whew, my brain's on overload. Studying for the bar exam is really tough."

Quinn murmured sympathetically.

"So," Marla glanced around the small room, "where's the hunk?"

"At the shop. McLeish! Bring that to me." Quinn swiftly rescued the stuffed monkey Gabe had given her from the cat's greedy clutches. "Poor, nameless monkey." She smoothed its bedraggled pelt and chided, "Don't be mean to the monkey."

McLeish looked up with his protuberant black eyes and purred—the picture of innocence.

"That cat's a monster," Marla offered.

"No, he's not. He just wants to play." She sat the stuffed toy on the end table and went back to her sentry of the empty driveway.

Amazing how in just a few short days she'd become so used to having Gabe around the house. In fact, she'd come to rely on his presence more and more.

As though reading her thoughts, Marla said, "Seems funny when Gabe's not here. I've never seen a man with more to offer. Besides being mega-gorgeous, he's a nurse, housekeeper, cat-sitter, shopkeeper."

And exciter of the senses, Quinn thought. She grinned at her friend. She didn't know who was more beguiled by Gabe's overt masculine charisma—she or Marla.

Marla was right, though. Since Gabe had moved in shortly over a week ago, the very walls of the small cabin seemed to strain with the burden of sheltering his boundless vitality.

Between Gabe, McLeish, and frequently—very frequently—Marla, the little house fairly burgeoned with life.

Although Quinn had lived alone for years, she surprisingly found Gabe a very pleasurable addition to her household. She had expected a period of adjustment—irritation at finding his towel on the bathroom floor, or catching him drinking milk from the carton.

But, no, Gabriel Hunter brought a sense of fullness, completeness, to her life that she hadn't even realized was missing. He fit right in. Except, she thought with a fond smile, that he still wore his long johns. Every now and then she'd get a peek of white showing beneath his shirt sleeve at the cuff.

"I know one thing," Marla continued. "If that man was mine, I wouldn't let him out of bed—to go to work or anyplace else! Of course, maybe you're way ahead of me. I mean, every time I come over here you're smiling and humming. You got anything to confide in your old pal, pal?"

Quinn's lip curved up in mock consternation. Marla was not afraid to broach any subject. Nothing was too personal to evade her scrutiny. And she was right in a way. Although Quinn's good humor didn't have anything to do with Gabe's sexual abilities, he *did* make her happy. She forgot her worries about the shop, about Daniel's convalescent care and, most of all, she forgot about being lonely.

She also tried, very hard, to forget about the reason they were together to begin with. Elvira's wretched will. How Quinn wished she'd never heard of that document. Any day now, the evaluation papers would be coming from the attorney's office. Papers that would ultimately take Gabe from her life.

"Oh, Marla," she moaned, fondling the cat's crimped ear. "What am I going to do about that damned will?"

"I told you what to do, tell Gabe everything."

"I can't do that, I promised the lawyer that I wouldn't say anything. Especially to Gabe." Quinn grumbled. "But it makes me feel so underhanded. Sneaky. What if Gabe does find out? What's he going to think?"

"Mrrrow." McLeish raised his smooshed-in face and gave her his opinion.

Marla pointed a chubby finger at Quinn. "He's going to think you're underhanded and sneaky. So, tell the man."

"I can't. Mr. Shaw was very explicit about that. If I break the confidence not only will I forfeit my bequest, but Gabe will lose his inheritance as well!"

Marla shook her head. "What's worse, losing the money or losing that wonderful man?"

Quinn stroked the cat's downy fur. "You don't understand. Gabe wants to expand his business but doesn't have the capital. He lost almost everything he owned in his divorce proceedings. Elvira's estate would give him another chance."

"Prrrr." The cat turned onto his back, allowing her the opportunity to rub his tummy.

"Quinn, if you don't tell him, and it comes out anyway, you know he's not going to believe it's *his* inheritance you were worried about."

"Oh, Marla, I've never had any money. Except for not being able to bring Daniel back home, I wouldn't care about losing that money. But I can't be the one to deny Gabe his rightful inheritance.''

She got no argument from the cat or Marla on that issue.

"Oh the heck with it," Quinn muttered. "I'll just take one day at a time." She didn't see what else she could do; any ill-advised action could cost her Gabe and she couldn't bear that.

Marla stood up. "I've got to get back to the books. But take my advice, old buddy. It's free. Tell him everything.''

Quinn nodded. "I'll think about it.''

"Yeah, you keep procrastinating and you're going to think yourself out of one terrific guy!''

Quinn stared at the door that closed behind her friend. She knew Marla was probably right—but what if she wasn't? What if, because of her, Gabe lost his inheritance? Wouldn't he blame her?

Quinn turned the puzzle over and over in her mind, like a Rubik's Cube whose solution evaded her.

She had to have more time. Time to think about the will and time to explore her feelings about Gabe. Time was also running out.

With each passing day, days that would eventually take him away, she learned to appreciate a new facet of Gabe's multi-layered personality.

He was wonderful company. A self-generating dynamo, he paced the floor, arms waving, talking endlessly of his ideas, plans for his business future and talking thoughtfully about his past.

Slowly, Gabe Hunter was helping her let go of the past. Teaching her that she didn't have to be serious and level-headed *all* the time. Quinn was finding the world didn't come crashing down around her ears if she laughed aloud.

One morning she had watched from the front window as Gabe laboriously raked leaves from the front yard. Then, like a little boy, he ran and jumped into the pile, scattering the colorful leaves all over the ground again. Picking broken bits of twigs and dead grass from his sweater, he grinned and started raking again.

Quinn snapped back to the present as, at last, the red car pulled into its accustomed spot. Her heart lurched in anticipation.

"Look, McLeish," she lifted the chunky red cat onto her lap and pointed out the window. "He's home. Look."

McLeish didn't act the slightest bit impressed.

A moment later the front door opened and Gabe's now-familiar tread sounded from the foyer. McLeish uncurled his chunky mass from his favorite spot by the fireplace and sauntered to the front door.

Soon Gabe's lean form appeared in the doorway. "Hi, honey, I'm home!"

Quinn looked up, startled. Although Gabe was, as usual, clowning around, that had sounded so . . . so right, somehow.

She was definitely getting used to having him around the house.

With a smile of welcome, she went back to the fresh green beans she was snapping.

"Mmmm. Something smells good." He squeezed her shoulder and flopped into the recliner. "But you're not supposed to be roaming around cooking."

"I used my crutches. And sat while I peeled potatoes. It doesn't require a lot of walking to throw a roast into the oven. Besides, I was bored."

"So you resorted to cooking? That's not kind, Quinn. I saw some eggs you charred once, remember?"

She threw a green bean at him. He picked it up from his lap and bit into the raw veggie.

"Needs salt. Where, by the way, is that four-footed monster?"

"He was right here a minute ago. I don't know where . . ."

She broke off as a mysterious thud sounded from the kitchen.

"Uh-oh," they chimed in unison.

Gabe had barely gotten to his feet to check out McLeish's latest calamity when the pudgy feline bounded into the room. Parking his posterior on the sofa beside Quinn, he dropped something from his mouth and nudged it in her direction.

With a frown, she reached over to retrieve the treasure he'd presented to her. "What's this, McLeish? Have you brought Quinnie a . . . oh, my God!" She squealed and leapt to her feet, heedless of the pain that raced through her ankle.

"Quinn! What's going on?" Gabe took two long strides to her side.

"Yuck! I touched it," she shrieked. "Gabe, get it."

"What? What is it?"

"Ooooh. It's a mouse. And I think it's still alive. Do something, Gabe. I hate those things."

He stepped back and cleared his throat. "I'm . . . uh, I'm not too fond of them either."

"Well, you're the man—this is your job."

He inched over and looked at the creature, dazed but still squirming on the sofa. "That was a very sexist remark, Quinn. I'm surprised at you."

Hopping on one foot, she dodged spilled green beans, and leaned on his arm for support. "Do something. Get rid of it."

Drawing a deep breath, Gabe advanced. "Okay, sit down on the recliner. I'll hand you the cat. And hold him. He's not apt to take kindly to my taking away the prize he brought you."

"Okay. But hurry." She hopped across the room and slumped into the leather chair.

Distaste obvious on his lean face, Gabe scooped the cat up and dropped him onto Quinn's lap.

"Okay now. The mouse," he was talking more to himself than to Quinn. "Something to pick it up with. Let's see . . ."

Spying a magazine next to the sofa, he snatched it up. He used it like a shovel, pushing it under the mouse's tiny body. With a couple of deft movements, he held the creature aloft. "Now what do I do with it?"

Quinn held onto her struggling charge with both hands. He had seen Gabe appropriate his bounty, and wasn't taking kindly to the theft. "Don't kill it!"

His black-fringed eyes widened in surprise. "I thought you hated them?"

"I do. But I don't want you to kill it. Just take it outside. But don't put it where McLeish will get it again."

"Yeah, right," Gabe muttered, as he carefully balanced the magazine holding the frightened mouse and made his way to the front door.

It was dark by the time Gabe came back into the room, drying his hands on a dishtowel. "Mission accomplished. Thank goodness, in a few weeks our temporary joint-custody of that demonic animal will be terminated."

"I think you're forgetting one thing, though."

"Oh?" He winced, as if not sure he wanted to hear her response.

And with good reason, she thought. "Gabe, when this is over—one of us is going to get stuck with permanent custody."

"He likes you best," Gabe promptly stated.

"Maybe. But he's *your* inheritance."

He threw the dishtowel over his shoulder and started gathering green beans off the carpet. "I've got a good idea. I'll race you for custody. Hundred-yard dash."

Quinn pointed to her bandaged extremity. "You wouldn't be trying to take unfair advantage, would you?"

He pointed both forefingers at his chest. "*Moi?*"

"Yeah, you. So did you dispose of our little furry friend?"

"As ordered. Quinn, I absolutely *hate* mice and rats. Now snakes, grizzly bears, zebras . . . I'll show you a tough macho man if you want me to tame one of them. But mice—yuck!''

Quinn shuddered. She could certainly echo his sentiments. "Was it . . . dead?"

Gabe shook his head. "No, perked right up when I let him down."

"What took you so long?"

Gabe shrugged. "For a rodent, that little guy had personality. He looked so scared, I didn't want to drop him off in your yard. Figured McLeish would snag him again. So I carried him to that empty field down the street."

Quinn stared. That empty field was over a half mile away. "You mean you carried that . . . mouse . . . balanced on a magazine all the way down there?"

A sheepish look on his face, he admitted, "No, when he started coming around, he was scrabbling all over that magazine. I was afraid he'd fall off. That would be a long fall for a critter that small."

"So what did you do?"

Gabe shrugged again, and turned his head. "Picked him up and carried him. What else was I going to do?"

"With your bare hands?"

"What else? I washed them twice since I got back."

"Gabe?" Quinn's voice was soft, melodic. "Would you help me up?"

"What?"

Ruefully, she grasped the significance of his amazed expression. For the past few days she'd grown so weary of being confined and virtually helpless, that every time Gabe had offered the slightest assistance she had snapped and snarled like a fettered pit bull. The man was a saint—she'd have stuffed a sock in his mouth if their situations were reversed.

Smiling brightly, she pointed. "My crutches are over there."

"Sure." He bent down so that she could drape one arm

across his wide shoulders. Then, he wrapped his arm around her slender waist and helped her up.

In that position, they walk-hopped to the sofa. But when Quinn sat down, she didn't loosen her grasp on Gabe's shoulder. Instead, she pulled him down beside her.

"What's this?" His eyebrows raised, charcoal exclamations of surprise.

She wrapped both arms around his neck and pulled his head closer. "I just wanted to tell you that what you did was wonderful. A very heroic deed."

Gabe snorted. "Heroic? Getting rid of a mouse? Methinks you're given to flights of exaggeration."

"Now don't be modest." She ruffled her fingers through the crisp black hair that just grazed his collar.

His voice was an octave lower when he spoke. "I was almost as afraid of the damned thing as you were."

Quinn shook her head, denying his disclaimer. "Heroism is when you're afraid of something, yet do it anyway. It took a lot of courage to pick up that . . . critter, and hold it for a half mile. You saved his life. Maybe mine, too."

Gabe looked away, but not before she saw the sheepish grin of pleasure brighten his features. He looked back. "You're serious?"

"Absolutely. You're my hero."

"You're ditsy. But I adore you anyway."

Gabe pulled back and stared into the depths of her eyes. His hand soothed her brow and brushed the strands of auburn silk from her face. "You know, I've waited a very long time for someone like you," he whispered.

She'd waited for him all her life, but she couldn't say the words aloud. She trembled with fear. Fear of what this moment could lead to. Fear of being hurt. Fear of hurting.

So she said nothing.

"I mean it," he insisted. "You know the best and the worst of me. And I know that what we have between us is real and honest. I don't have much to offer you, but . . ."

She raised her fingers to his lips, to still the flow of words that, if uttered, would surely come between them.

"Shhh. I don't need you to say . . ."

"I need to say it."

But she couldn't bear to hear it. Words of honesty and truth. While all she could offer in return were lies.

"Gabe, this is all happening so fast. We need to take time. To know each other before we . . ."

"More time, Quinn? We've already wasted so much."

"I know, but you don't know anything about me. Not really."

"I know all I need to about you." He kissed the tip of her nose. "I know that you're kind, and generous, and sexy as hell and . . . just about perfect."

"No," she said softly, pushing him away. She sat up and brushed her fiery tresses from her moist brow. "I'm not perfect, Gabe. Don't ever think that, you'll be disappointed."

He leaned back, his golden eyes flecked with confusion. "Quinn? What is it? Is there something you want to tell me? Something you think I should know?"

She closed her eyes and sighed. *No, Gabe, something I'm so frightened you won't understand when you find out.*

Opening her eyes, she whispered, hating the lie, "No. I just want you to be sure. I don't want either of us to be hurt again."

Her fingers pushed an errant lock of black hair from his forehead.

Blowing out a deep breath, Gabe stared at her for a long moment. "All right, Quinn. I promised not to push you. So we'll take it a little slower."

Seeing the hurt and confusion in his eyes, her passion died like withered fruit left too long on the vine. She only knew she couldn't give herself freely with this secret standing between them.

Realizing the conversation had reached its dismal end, Gabe stood up and walked to the doorway. Scooping McLeish into his arms, he turned in the doorway. "The ball's in your court now, you let me know when you're ready. I'll be around."

*   *   *

After dinner, Quinn sat on the sofa, stuffing the ample bosom of a Mrs. Claus scarecrow for the Christmas theme. Gabe was leaning back in the leather recliner, his portable computer whirring in his lap.

The evening had been tense, as they both tried to find avenues for communication that wouldn't remind them of the aborted encounter earlier in the afternoon. Several times, she had caught Gabe looking at her from over his lap-top, looking as though he wanted to talk about the invisible wall she had erected between them. But when she quickly avoided her gaze, he would clear his throat and comment about some trivial issue that neither of them cared about.

He looked up again. Taking a deep breath, he forced a smile. "I got three more orders for Santa today."

"You're kidding?"

The crooked grin she'd grown so fond of creased his lean face as his normal good humor was restored. "Would I kid you, kiddo? No, remember the woman I ran into at the craft show—Madelyne Parker?"

An icy wind swept through Quinn at the mention of the woman's name. "I remember."

"Well, remember I told you she was a buyer for a large chain of department stores?"

Quinn nodded mutely. She didn't trust her voice.

"Anyway, I showed her some Polaroids of your scarecrows and today she took the two elves and ordered three Santas. Paid in advance, I might add, and hinted she'd take as many as we could furnish. By the way, I think we should raise our prices by at least fifteen percent. You're under-valuing your labor."

Quinn laid Mrs. Claus facedown beside her on the sofa. "But I don't understand. I hadn't photographed the Christmas Crows yet."

"Oh, she came by the shop. We had a nice lunch."

I'll just bet you did. Quinn closed her eyes, choosing

her words with care. *I will not over-react. I will not over-react.* "She came all the way from Los Angeles for a few scarecrows?"

Gabe looked up from his flickering computer screen and smiled sheepishly. "We're old friends, remember?"

How could she forget? The damned woman kept popping up everywhere. But I will not over-react.

"Anyway," Gabe continued, "when she saw those holiday scarecrows, she grabbed up all we had on the spot."

"I told you that I wasn't planning on displaying the Christmas Crows until after Thanksgiving. How did she see them?"

Gabe turned off his computer and leaned back, lacing his fingers behind his head. "Well, I made a judgment call. I showed them to her. Normally, I agree—Christmas decorations after Thanksgiving. But you have a unique circumstance up here. Your handcrafted items are pretty labor-intensive. You need to get a head start. Particularly for people like Madelyne who needs to order *her* holiday stock now."

She over-reacted.

"I don't think that you should be making arbitrary decisions about my business without asking me first." *Especially when those decisions involve that woman.*

He frowned. "Did you really want me to call you, or come get you, to ask if we could sell five scarecrows? Madelyne is a potential goldmine for you, Quinn. I'd think you'd want to accommodate her as much as possible."

Quinn had to admit that he made a lot of sense, but she didn't care for the way he was disregarding her instructions. She also didn't care for the way Madelyne Parker kept showing up. This was *not* jealousy, she told herself. This was business. The Scarecrow Emporium was hers and she still had the right to dictate marketing policies.

"I think we should set up the holiday window right now," Gabe said.

"I'm not sure," she demurred, trying to get her mind

back on marketing strategy and off Madelyne Parker. Gabe might be the marketing genius but she wasn't sure he was right about speeding up the holiday displays. If she pushed the Christmas merchandise, wouldn't that knock a hole in her planned Halloween sales?

"Let me think about it," she said.

He shrugged. "Okay. But what do you think about the prices? Should I start re-marking the stock we already have?"

"I don't know," she shook her head in hesitation. In her opinion the merchandise was already pretty pricey for purely decorative items. "I don't want to price myself out of business."

He nodded. "True. And if your clientele were the locals you'd have a good point. But for people used to city premiums, your scarecrows are dirt cheap. Almost too inexpensive, in fact."

Was he implying that her products were too seedy for Madelyne's moneyed customers? "What do you mean?"

"You know that old adage about getting what you pay for? Well," he continued when she murmured an acknowledgment, "one of the oldest marketing ploys around is that when something isn't selling—raise the price."

"That doesn't make sense," she frowned.

Gabe explained. "Customers, especially customers who have the discretionary income to buy what-nots and doodads like you sell, want to feel like they're getting something unique. One of a kind. And you don't have one-of-a-kind prices. In fact, your prices imply mass-produced."

"I don't know, Gabe. It's hard enough to make ends meet with such a small business, I wouldn't want to run my customers off by charging too much. You've only been helping out a few days, I've been running that shop for two years. I know what I'm doing."

He set his computer on the floor and pulled the lever on the recliner, raising it upright. Heaving himself up, he crossed the room to stand directly in front of her. "What you're doing is being defensive about my suggestions. I would think you'd welcome my input. My clients pay a lot of money for my advice. I can't believe you'd just toss it away because it's free. In fact, your attitude proves my point."

"I'm *not* being defensive. I just don't know how you think you can learn the ins and outs of my business in such a short time."

"Why do you always treat me like a little boy playing games? For Pete's sake, Quinn, I'm a marketing consultant by trade."

"Sure, to huge corporations. This is a small business. And I don't think that my business methods have been so inadequate."

"I didn't say that! I was just offering suggestions of how you can broaden your customer base and vastly enhance your net sales. I thought you were in business to make money. Obviously, I was wrong. This is just a hobby for you. A way to stay hidden up here on this mountain so you won't have to face the big, bad world anymore." He threw his hands in the air and stalked out of the room.

Quinn picked up Mrs. Claus and continued filling her muslin body with straw. What did he know? Okay, maybe a lot. But she'd been doing fine before he came along.

And what did that crack mean about hiding out on the mountain? Just because she didn't care for the impersonal, hectic pace of city life didn't mean she was hiding out.

What did he know about her life anyway?

Nothing, she admitted. Nothing because she refused to take down that blasted wall and let him in. Because she was a coward.

Better a coward than broken-hearted.

She took a few furious tucks in Mrs. Claus' apron but soon gave up. Realizing she'd stitched the scarecrow's blouse to her own skirt, Quinn tossed it aside in disgust.

Leaning back against the sofa cushions, she closed her

eyes and sighed. Gabe had unknowingly struck her most vulnerable nerve: The nuts-and-bolts part of running a business.

Oh, her designs and workmanship were excellent, and she did an adequate job with the window displays. And, of course, handling simple tasks like ordering supplies and paying invoices presented no problem. The problem was that Quinn knew absolutely nothing about the finer points of retail sales—marketing.

She'd opened her boutique on a shoestring budget and realized now that she hadn't garnered enough merchandising knowledge before plunging in. It was only through blind luck and perseverance that she'd managed to hang onto the shop this long.

But why did it have to be Gabe who noticed and remarked on her shortcomings?

She hated to face it, but the truth was that she wanted to look flawless in his eyes, like she was a whiz at everything she tried. She didn't want him to be disappointed in her.

When had his opinion become so important, she asked herself, suddenly alert.

Why was *he* so important?

He's only everything you've always wanted in a man.

The realization dropped into her awareness with the force of a runaway elevator.

It was true. He was kind, considerate, sexy, witty and, yes, she admitted grudgingly, responsible. The way he had taken over and singlehandedly picked up the pieces of her life was remarkable. What was truly amazing was that she had managed so long without him.

But he was also only hers on a loan. In a few weeks, he'd claim his inheritance and resume his life in Del Mar. A life of elegant restaurants, beautiful women, and a high-powered job.

A life that didn't include her.

Well, he wasn't going to spend the next few weeks radically changing *her* life then strolling back to his playboy lifestyle, and leave her world topsy-turvy.

It was too late to pull her emotional attachment to Gabe back into line. She was severely attracted to the man. But she'd had physical attractions before. They never lasted. Nothing lasted.

She wouldn't be hurt again.

McLeish strolled into the room and vaulted onto her lap. "Oh, good. I needed somebody to talk to." She tossed the stuffed toy onto the coffee table. It reminded her too much of Gabe.

"You know what I like about you, McLeish? You always listen to me. Not like someone else I could name who stomps off and pouts when he doesn't get his way."

Quinn hated to admit, even to herself, how much she wanted to get up and follow Gabe down the hall. Tell him the truth. But if she couldn't make him understand about her role in the probate of Elvira's will, she'd lose him.

No. For once Quinn Rosetti was going to have some control over a situation.

She'd managed to operate her boutique with a minimal profit for two years. She'd manage a little longer and she'd do it without Gabriel Hunter's transient help. And without Madelyne Parker's snobbish clientele, either.

No one was going to change her store!

She had to draw the line somewhere.

TWELVE

By the next morning, Quinn's resolve had somewhat faded.

For one thing, it was an unseasonably warm day and Gabe had appeared at breakfast in denim cut-offs and T-shirt.

The cut-offs, without looking painted on, were form-fitting and hugged his dark, muscular thighs and high, taut backside.

He looked like a sculpture by Michelangelo, crafted of exquisite Italian marble. His well-developed chest boldly pressed against his white cotton T-shirt, proving the perfect counterpoint for the finely-honed planes of his abdominal muscles.

Then the image changed, took on life, as he lifted his arms to rummage through the cupboards. Stretching. Reaching. Straining the thin fabric to its limits. Quinn watched in fascination as the muscles along his shoulders and back bunched and rippled in a sensuous, undulating motion. As an artist, she had always found beauty in the human body. Gabe's was especially beautiful, she thought.

But her reaction was more than a simple detached admiration of the masculine form. Watching him, she felt that heated response that surged through her very being every time his thick black lashes flicked closed with butterfly softness. Or when he treated her to that crooked grin with those dazzling white teeth. Or even, or even just when his arm brushed against her breast when helping her in or out of the wheelchair.

While attending art school, Quinn had sketched her share of beautiful men. Many posed in the nude. She had spent hours studying every nuance of their well-formed bodies. These men were professional models—perfect in every manner. If she judged on looks alone, a good number were more physically perfect than Gabe. Yet, not once had she enjoyed the delicious arousal she felt when looking at him.

So what was it about Gabriel Hunter that was so different—so heart-stoppingly different—from other, more handsome, men?

The answer came to her as clearly as a trumpet call. It was more than sexual attraction. More than loneliness and long-ignored hormones. She was falling in love with him.

He turned around and caught her gaze. "Something wrong?"

His voice was still cold, distant. He'd not gotten over her rebuff of his advice from last night. Gabe was looking at her with an intensity that made her feel transparent—as though he could read every thought, every quiver of emotion.

"No," she mumbled. "Nothing's wrong."

"Are you sure?" He looked down, then skimmed the palms of his hands over his well defined seat. "I haven't ripped my shorts or something, have I?"

He knew perfectly well she wasn't thinking about torn clothing. She was thinking about that impenetrable barrier that she had built, brick by brick, and placed between them.

Quinn bit her lip. Taking his cue from her, Gabe had gone back to hiding his true feelings behind a smoke screen of jocularity. Yesterday he had let himself be vulnerable, today he was taking no chances.

Well, neither was she. Gabe Hunter was just a temporary condition—like a bad case of the measles. A high fever in the beginning. Followed by a miserable itch. Then, finally, a long recuperative period until all the symptoms faded.

McLeish made his first appearance of the morning, by jumping onto the kitchen table and dropping Nameless Monkey onto the open butter dish.

"Get down, you mangy creature." Gabe picked him up and set him forcefully on the floor then retrieved the bedraggled toy and wiped its face with a paper napkin.

"Just because you're still mad at me is no reason to take it out on the poor cat!" Quinn snarled as she reached down to pick up the feisty feline.

"I'm *not* still mad at you," Gabe snarled back. "I wasn't mad in the first place—just frustrated." He ran splayed fingers through his thick, coal-dark hair, punctuating his tension.

"Puh-lease! Don't give me that old ploy about your pent-up sexual energy making you edgy. We weren't fighting about sex."

He slammed his palm on the kitchen table, causing the salt and pepper shakers to bounce. "For your information, I wasn't *talking* about sex. There are other kinds of frustration, you know," he muttered sarcastically. "But it's encouraging to know you're at least thinking about our love life—or the lack of it."

"Gabe, I thought we agreed to take it slow? Give ourselves time?"

He stalked over to the refrigerator and poured a large glass of milk. Swallowing it down in one long draught, he wiped the white moustache from his face with the back of his hand and leaned against the counter, eyeing her intently. When he spoke, his voice was calmer, as if his anger had been replaced with a deep sadness. "We agreed, Quinn, because you didn't give me much choice."

Oh, so now it was all *her* fault. Anger glittered in her

black fringed eyes as she snapped back. "You're twisting this all around! Our argument last night was about your taking over my business."

"No, our argument was about not trusting. In or out of bed. Quinn, you know my ex was a gold digger . . . but I don't automatically expect every other woman to be one. Especially you. You see, I'm capable of trusting you. Why can't you let go of whatever . . . or whoever . . . hurt you in the past and trust me, too?" His voice broke off abruptly and he turned quickly toward the sink to rinse his empty glass.

But not before Quinn saw the dark cloud of pain shadow his eyes.

Gabe busied himself opening cupboards, allowing time for the tension in the room to fade somewhat. Quinn wanted to argue with him, force him to believe that she did trust him—but she knew that would be a lie so she remained silent. She wanted to believe in Gabe, desperately. Wanted to believe that he wouldn't use her. But she was so afraid to break down that protective shell she'd spent so long developing.

Perhaps with a little more time . . .

"What's that animal caterwauling about?" Gabe's voice, with its forced normalcy, cut into her confusing thoughts.

"He's probably hungry." Quinn scratched the cat behind his floppy ear and lowered him to the floor. "I forgot to feed him last night."

"I'll do it." He pulled a tin of cat food from the cupboard and spooned it into the cat's dish.

After a proper wait, the cat deigned to nibble on his breakfast.

Gabe looked at Quinn who was sitting with her chin cupped in her hand, staring into space. "Are you all right?"

"Yes, I was just thinking."

He leaned over her shoulder to place a bowl of cereal on the table. His nearness was stifling.

"Sleep well?" he asked.

"Fine," she lied. The bed she'd slept in most of her life suddenly felt too large. Too empty. "What about you?"

He hitched up a kitchen chair and lifted his coffee mug to his lips. "I didn't sleep worth a damn either."

They were both silent for a moment, then both spoke at once.

"Quinn, I'm sorry . . ."

"Gabe, I was a real . . ."

He set the mug down and reached to cover her hand with his own large one. "I was acting like a jerk. I shouldn't have pushed so hard. I'm sorry."

Her hand tingled beneath his touch, sending another charge of electricity up her arm and into her chest. Her heart lurched and throbbed like the frenetic beat of wild, *salsa* music.

Her voice, when she found it, sounded weak and wobbly to her ear. "That . . . that's okay. I was a little defensive."

Gabe ran his thumb over the top of her hand, again causing her pulse to skitter with little currents of excitement. Her flesh shivered with longing. She wanted to be covered with his touch, smothered by his lips, drowned by his desire. . . .

She was yanked from her delicious fantasy as Gabe lifted his hand from hers and crossed the space between them. He kneeled beside her chair and buried his hands in the luxurient fullness of her red hair, still tousled from sleep.

"Quinn, I wouldn't hurt you for the world," he whispered, then pulled her close until their breaths mingled. Slowly, with an exquisite sweetness, he brought his mouth to hers and claimed her lips with a tenderness that made her melt against him.

Her heart swelled in her chest and pounded against her rib cage as she returned the gentle pressure. She felt as if she were floating on a huge puffy cloud, high above the world, existing only for the taste of his mouth.

She wrapped her arms around his neck, basking in the glory of his clean, masculine scent. Her fingers found the short crisp hairs at his nape, then the unexpectedly smooth skin just below. Wriggling in her chair, she arched toward him, needing to feel him against her throbbing breast.

Then, with the same gentleness, he pulled away.

"I said I wouldn't push you," he murmured huskily, "and I won't."

Please, her tortured flesh seemed to scream, *push me. Take the decision away from me.* But she couldn't force the words to her lips, so with a deep shuddering sigh, she leaned back in her chair as Gabe arose and returned to his.

He rubbed the chiseled edge of his chin, and focused his eyes on the wall behind her. Finally, he cleared his throat and spoke with slow deliberation, continuing their conversation as if there had been no interruption. No intimate kiss. "I guess I thought of your store like one of my client's businesses. Poured all of my energy into it and couldn't understand that you don't move at the same obsessive pace I do."

"You miss your business, don't you?"

He thought about it for a moment. "I guess I miss the excitement, but I sure don't miss that frenzied pace of city life. Hunting for parking places. Freeway jams. Lines everywhere. And of course, the biggie, traffic lights."

She smiled, forgetting her earlier pique and banishing the memory of his lips, although she could still feel their warmth on her mouth.

Forcing herself to respond to his attempt to return to safer ground, she said, "Idyllwild must be quite a treat then. Not a single traffic light."

"Yeah," he agreed, "I like this little burg. No crime, no rush hour traffic. Perfect. If only . . . if only there was a little excitement around here."

They burst into laughter at his nonsensical logic. Quinn was so relieved that he seemed to have forgotten their harsh words the night before that she decided that she had mentally blown the whole thing out of proportion. It was true, she acknowledged ruefully, she had been looking for a fight. Looking for a reason to write off this budding relationship.

The golden rule in reverse—do unto others before they do unto you.

She must have been right, she decided a few days later when she noticed that Gabe had offered no more suggestions on ways to improve the Emporium's cash flow.

They were in his car, on the way to Dr. Johnson's for the re-check of Quinn's ankle. It was a comfortable kind of afternoon, Quinn thought, as she watched a gray squirrel scamper across the road doing some last minute nut gathering.

It had been a quiet, companionable kind of week, Quinn mused.

Madelyne Parker's name had not been mentioned since their fight. Quinn had tried to push thoughts of the blonde woman to the background, without success. At least once a day she was plagued by a vision of Gabe enjoying an intimate meal with Madelyne—candlelight flickering softly. Quinn hoped she scorched those impossibly-long eyelashes leaning over the candle.

Ruefully, she was forced to admit that Gabe couldn't be spending his free time with Madelyne or anyone else. When he wasn't at the Scarecrow Emporium, his time was spent either entering figures into his computer or telephoning his clients.

Or taking care of you, she reminded herself. And he had certainly been diligent and uncomplaining about his nursing duties.

They arrived at Dr. Johnson's office. Gabe helped her from the car and she hobbled on her crutches into the waiting room.

"Mmm-hmm," the doctor said a short time later. He probed her injured ankle with fingers not nearly as gentle as Gabe's. "How's that feel?"

"Okay."

"Mmm-hmm. And how about here?"

"Ow. Still a little tender."

"That's to be expected. But, all in all, I'd say you're healing admirably. Someone must be taking pretty good care of you."

She looked up at Gabe, who was leaning in his accustomed spot against the lurid chart of internal organs. "Yes, he's taking very good care of me."

"And how are you doing, Mr. Hunter?"

Gabe smiled indulgently. "Just fine, sir."

Another positive for his evaluation. Very respectful of his elders. Rare today. She knew Daniel had noticed and appreciated the way Gabe deferred to him.

Ah-ha! That's what she'd call Nameless Monkey—Daniel Two. She couldn't wait to tell Gabe, he'd love it.

"Quinn?"

She started, realizing the doctor was addressing her. "I'm sorry, what did you say?"

"I said we need to start a program of exercise. But only for a very limited time each day, Quinn," the doctor warned, handing her a photocopied set of instructions on appropriate exercises. "Let's start building those muscles gradually. Five minutes in the morning and five minutes in the afternoon for the first day. Then each day you can increase the time by five minutes. Got it?"

"I'll see she sticks to the schedule," Gabe asserted.

Quinn resisted the urge to kick him in the shin with her good foot. She didn't need his kibitzing. She could follow simple instructions.

"Good." Dr. Johnson continued. "I'd say in another ten days, you'll be back to full power."

That pronouncement made her feel like she'd been caught in an ice storm. Cold all over. But especially cold inside.

So that was it. In ten days Gabe would be leaving. Back to the excitement of his city life. Oh, they'd see each other occasionally for the transfer of McLeish's custody. But in ten days, she'd be alone again.

The ride home was unusually quiet. The rare snippets of conversation were strained, unnatural comments about the approaching rain storm the weatherman was forecasting.

Halfway to the cabin, the first specks of moisture made a polka-dot pattern on the windshield. By the time Gabe turned into her yard, the driving rain was sluicing down in solid sheets.

"Looks like we're in for a good one," he observed, opening the car door.

"You're right," she shouted over the storm's roar. "Maybe you should bring in some more firewood before it all gets wet. Sometimes these late fall storms are real doozies. The power goes out. If we get too much run-off down the mountains, some of the roads get flooded. We may need the light and the heat from the fireplace. We could get rained in."

Gabe waggled his dark eyebrows, now sparkling with specks of water, like drops of sterling. "I could live with that."

A shiver ran up her spine. So could she. Quinn couldn't imagine anything more enticing than curling up all warm and comfy before a fire with Gabe. While outside a wonderful rain storm raged.

"Well, here goes!" Pulling the collar of his jacket up over his head like a hood, Gabe bolted from the car's sanctuary and ran to open the passenger door.

Because they had returned the wheelchair to Dr. Johnson, Quinn had to brave the insistent rain to get to the dry haven of the cabin.

"Be careful," Gabe admonished as the tip of her crutch slipped on the wet ground. Quinn's front yard was rapidly turning into an enormous mud bath.

"Here, take my arm." He pulled off his jacket and draped it around her like a shield, protecting her from the storm's fury.

Finally, they made it to the shelter of the covered porch.

Hustling her inside, he threw kindling into the fireplace. Soon, a sizzling blaze took the chill from the room.

"Gotta leave you alone for a while, babe." He pulled on his well-worn parka and started for the door.

"Where are you going in this mess?"

"More firewood, m'dear. We've ambiance to maintain around here." With a broad wink, he disappeared into the violent tempest.

Quinn leaned on her crutches, cozy and warm in front of the fire. How had she ever thought that Gabe was self-centered and irresponsible? Although he was a little high-handed on occasion, the very idea of him manipulating and using her was . . . simply ludicrous.

A twinge of conscience reminded her that if anyone was guilty of half-lies, it was she. Quinn cringed, shutting out the little voice that warned her to tell Gabe the truth. He'd understand. Wouldn't he?

Of course, he would, she tried to convince herself. After all, he'd already seen her acting suspicious, moody, accusing, grouchy—traits most men would find less than endearing. With his typical crooked grin, Gabe had accepted her flaws without complaint.

She closed her eyes and inhaled the ambiance he'd vowed to preserve; mountain air, a crackling blaze and a fifty-pound heart wrapped up in a beautiful hunk. If she could purr, she'd drown out McLeish, Quinn chuckled to herself.

The front door burst open and Gabe came in and dropped an armload of oak logs onto the hearth. He straightened up and caught the amusement lighting Quinn's lovely face.

"You look like you're having a good time without me. That's against the rules." A tiny smile bent the corners of Gabe's mouth up. His eyes flashed with a fire of their own.

Danger! Her mind picked up his message but she was too satiated in the suddenly electric atmosphere to listen.

Her breath caught, held and forced her to raise her face to gaze straight into the soul of the most delightful person she'd ever met. And he was with her. Alone. Now. In their private mountain retreat. Together. For the duration of the storm.

The moment of reckoning had arrived. Quinn knew they could no longer ignore this storm of their own that had been growing in intensity since the second they'd met.

Her emotions shifted back and forth between surrender and retreat.

Gabe solved the problem. As if reading her mind, he stood up, discarded her crutches and swept Quinn up in his arms. "Enough games, Quinn. Enough waiting. This is our night."

Quinn didn't miss the implied plan. The suddenness of his confident statement caused her breath to skip. Before she could turn the moment into one of self-evaluation, Gabe set her gently on the couch.

"Thank you very . . ."

His soft lips ended Quinn's good manners as Gabe entwined his long fingers into her damp auburn curls. "Let's not be so formal." He took her face in both hands and peered with a passion-filled intensity that gave his eyes a smoky glaze.

Quinn couldn't speak. Or breathe. Or stop the growing billows of sensation fluttering through her heart, filling her body with a quickening of desire.

"Gabe." She wanted to say love words that could express how she felt. "Gabe, I want you . . . to . . ." Clouds of yearning smothered her thinking processes. Without looking away, she reached for his face. The slight growth of his beard enhanced the touch, she pressed to amplify the thrill.

He bent over and kissed her fingers, one at a time.

With each touch of his lips her storm grew. The muscles of his neck tensed with sexual energy. She had to kiss that hollow spot between his neck and shoulder.

She buried her face against his neck, drinking in the delectable male scent that was uniquely his.

The heat of his skin released the first bolt of lightning.

Thousands of tiny charges crackled through her body, spreading the delight of his touch.

A moan escaped Gabe's lips as he responded by opening the top button on her silk blouse.

His lips brushed the hollow of her neck.

He lifted his head and smiled, the dearest, sexiest smile she had ever seen. "Are you sure, Quinn? Very sure?"

She couldn't talk, he had stolen her ability to vocalize with his marauding lips. Her eyes widened in surprise as she heard herself murmur, "I . . . I've never been more certain about anything in my life."

"I'm glad. Very glad. Tonight I want to shut out this storm, shut out the world and make love to you. Tomorrow we'll be sensible and analyze our relationship and fret about the future, but tonight . . . tonight is ours and we're going to make it last a lifetime."

As if in a trance, she watched as his fingers raised to her face, caressing her cheek, then trailed slowly, tantalizingly down her throat.

He slid his hand to the back of her neck, burrowing in her thick, auburn tresses. With a deep groan, he drew her mouth to his.

Quinn sighed in ecstasy. His lips were lush, sensual. Incredibly soft against hers. Gabe encircled her in his arms and began kissing her more deeply. Each thrust of his tongue seduced her with its provocative seeking. Quinn's breath lurched. Her senses reeled crazily, out of control, until she was mesmerized by the sweet taste of his lips.

She slid her arms up his back, pulling him close until her breasts were crushed against his chest. Her nipples prodded the thin silk blouse, proud emblems of her arousal.

She wanted their kiss to go on forever, to contain them in this moment, but her body seemed to have a will of its own. Wanting, no, demanding more.

Like a fire burning out of control, the passion ignited by his kiss spread throughout her body until it found the white-hot center of her femininity. She shifted her hips.

Twitched. Squirmed. Snuggled against him until she was singed by the hard heat that proclaimed his arousal to be as strong as her own.

Yes, she wanted to go on kissing him, but Quinn knew that finally, she was ready to give. And receive.

Gabe drew back and looked at her. His voice, strange and raspy, murmured, "You're the most beautiful, most desirable woman I've ever met. Never, ever, has anyone made me feel like you do. I want to hold you forever. I want to make love with you until you cry with joy. I want . . . oh!"

He broke off suddenly, burying his lips in the downy softness of her hair. "Quinn, Quinn, I've wanted you, needed you for so long . . ."

"I know," she murmured. "I think I wanted you the moment I laid eyes on you."

He lifted his head until his pale eyes, hooded with passion, were looking deep into hers. "Then let's not waste another moment."

Taking her hand, he led her into the bedroom.

Wordlessly, he ushered her to the bed and stood facing her, his face burnished with an internal fire that took her breath.

He ran a long, tapered finger along her jaw line. Down the side of her neck until, with a tortured groan, he dropped his hand to the open neck of her blouse. His hand trailed along the edge of the fabric, teasing her tender flesh, sending hot rushes of desire racing through her body.

Lowering his head, he kissed her deeply while his hand deftly opened the remaining buttons, exposing her wispy bra. Then, his questing fingers slipped beneath the fragile silk fabric. He gently caressed her breast, his fingertip finding and toying with the sensitive aureole, then tenderly rubbing her throbbing nipple.

Smoothing her hands up the broad expanse of his chest, Quinn pried open the buttons on his shirt, needing to feel his naked skin against her own. Finally, the last button released, she pushed aside his shirt, gliding her palms along the firm planes of his heaving chest, down to the taut muscles of his stomach. Her tongue sought and defined the sculptured muscles of his chest.

At her touch, Gabe's kisses grew hungrier, so hungry that they made her shudder in luxurious anticipation. Her entire being existed only for his touch. He softly moved his lips across her responding nipples. Even the sound of their rustling garments carried the aura of sensuality to new heights. Deep inside, in the very core of her desire, Quinn felt the delicious beginnings of a dull throbbing that wanted, no, demanded, Gabe.

She almost cried aloud when he pulled away from her long enough to shed his shirt. He touched her waistband, then, as if freed by a magician, her restrictive outer clothing fell away. With an enticing slowness, his fingers slipped beneath the silky wisp of her bra, sliding the strap down her shoulder.

Releasing the front-fastener, he liberated her breasts from the confining bra.

Cupping her face in his hands, he breathed, "I love you Quinn. Totally and completely." His mouth descended on hers, in a kiss of incredible sweetness, as he gently lowered her onto the bed.

Quinn's heart sang with joy. He loved her. Of all the women in the world, Gabe Hunter loved her.

Gabe raised up on the edge of the bed. His eyes dropped, sweeping the length of her body. "Beautiful. So very, very beautiful," he whispered.

Then, slowly, erotically, he slipped his hands inside her waistband and rolled her panties down her legs. For a moment, she felt vulnerable, exposed in her nudity. But then, as his mouth nibbled at her ankle, Quinn forgot her shyness and gave herself completely to the hypnotic sensations coursing through her.

All of her senses were heightened beyond belief. She

could feel the whisper of his beard lightly grazing her skin as he kissed his way back up her legs. Hear the huskiness of his breathing as it filled the room like a symphony. Her insides were liquid. She was a burbling cauldron of sensuality, about to boil over.

Gabe's lips caressed her knees as his hands gently widened the vee of her legs. Higher, higher his mouth nuzzled her inner thighs then settled at the damp cradle of her femininity. Her hips churned, thrusting upward. Seeking him with a need that threatened to consume her. Grasping the luxuriant softness of his hair, she drew him up.

"Please," she whispered, "please, I need . . ."

His mouth covered hers, then pulled away as he began kissing her breasts.

His lips played along her throat, his flattened palm pressing against the mound of her womanhood, his darting fingers teasing her moistness.

I want him. I want him. I want him. Swirling need captured her mind, burying rational thought.

Outside their world, the rainstorm's ferocity mounted, battering the small cabin with its wrath. She didn't hear it. Lightning flashes erupted. She didn't notice.

Giving in to the thunderous rumblings raging within her, Quinn lived only for the moment.

The throbbing between her legs had become an exquisite agony. She groaned with her need. "Now, Gabe, please . . ."

Quickly, he removed the rest of his clothes and stood before her for a moment. Fully aroused, his naked body looked like a glorious statue from antiquity, somehow come to life. She couldn't have imagined a man could be so . . . so beautiful.

At last, he lowered down, covering her body with his, fitting himself perfectly against her softness.

Her hips arched to meet him, desperate for the feel of him inside her.

Gabe calmed her trembling lips with his in a deep,

penetrating kiss that sought out and dismissed the last vestiges of her restraint. Quinn's tongue probed the sweetness of his mouth, eagerly matching his quest with her own.

"Oh, Gabe, I . . . I've never felt . . ."

"Hush, my darling," he stilled her with another kiss, igniting the few remaining nerve endings in her body.

Quinn tossed her head and pulled him to her, no longer able to withstand the onslaught of desire that threatened to consume her.

His hands moved to her hips and she raised to meet him. At last, he entered her, filling her yearning need. She wrapped her legs around him and moved to the rhythm of his body. Thrusting. Accepting. Melding together in an ancient love-dance created anew by their love—unique and precious.

Gabe's breathing grew more labored and she knew his passion was mounting. Her heart leaped at the perfection of their union. She loved making love with him, loved the feel of his expanse inside her. Quinn knew this was the moment she had been born for.

At last, as the thundering ache between her legs expanded to an exquisite torture, she felt the exalted rush of release.

Gabe thrust harder, until she felt the shudder of rapture race through his body. They collapsed together, their sweat-dampened bodies deliciously spent.

THIRTEEN

The shrill cry of the telephone awoke them. Sometime in the night Gabe had pulled the blanket over them and they had fallen into an exhausted, satiated sleep.

"What time is it," Quinn asked drowsily. Her lips were still swollen from Gabe's kisses. She was drained. Bereft of energy, but luxuriating in the afterglow.

Gabe looked at the bedside clock and groaned. "Too early to get up, that's for sure."

The phone rang again.

With a muttered curse, he struggled to sit up. "I'll get it."

Picking up the receiver, he croaked, "Hello. Oh, hi, Marla." He scowled dramatically and raised his dark eyebrows. "Quinn? No, I don't think she's out of bed yet."

Quinn punched him in the side with her elbow.

"Ouch! What did you say, Marla? No, no nothing's wrong. Yep, we survived the storm." He glanced at Quinn and winked. "In fact, I'd say we survived it pretty well."

Quinn rolled her eyes and pulled the blanket over her head. With all of his double entendres, Marla would be over here in a flash poking around for the juicy details. Details that were a secret bond between them.

But it was no use hoping for continued solitude. Since Marla's decision that Gabe was the most wonderful man on earth, she didn't know the meaning of the word private.

"Hmmm, that's a little early, Marla. That storm kept us up all night." He winked broadly at Quinn over the receiver.

Quinn groaned and threw a bed pillow at Gabe. It missed and fell to the floor with a soft plop.

She heard him tell Marla that they'd expect her for coffee around ten, then he hung up the receiver.

"Your buddy," he said, as he sunk back under the warm blanket, "seems to believe something is going on over here."

"Now, whatever would give her that idea?"

He cuddled against her rump. "I don't know, but give me a minute and I'll see if I can come up with something."

"That's crude, Hunter."

He pulled her rumpled hair away from her neck and kissed the sensitive flesh. "You, my dear Ms. Rosetti, have a dirty mind."

With a bawdy chuckle, she turned into his arms. "Yeah, and you love it."

She smacked his rump through the tangled sheets. "Well, Hunter, since you've invited company over for coffee, I'd say we'd better hit the shower and get dressed."

"Huh-uh," he shook his tousled head. "Our company's not coming until ten—that's two empty hours we need to fill somehow. Got any ideas?"

"No, but I'll bet you can think of something."

"I'll take that as a challenge."

He leaned over and pulled the sheet, exposing her naked breasts. Using his tongue like a lethal weapon, he slowly licked her quivering flesh. His darting tongue flicked the underside of her heaving mounds, and slid upward, sweetly torturing her sensitized nipples.

Raising his head, he murmured, "I think, Ms. Rosetti, that if you have your heart set on that shower that we'd better get going."

"I think you're right," she whispered, clasping his head between her palms and forcing his questing lips from her bosom.

"Okay," he groaned, "I surrender. To the showers."

He pulled her from the bed's comfort and draped an arm around her shoulders as he led her to the bathroom.

"I generally shower alone," Quinn protested half-heartedly.

He lifted her palm to his lips. "If you think I'm going to let you out of my sight for even one minute, you're crazy."

"In that case, you can wash my back."

Treating her to a lascivious grin, he offered with mock-lechery, "My pleasure, m'lady. I'll be happy to wash your back, your feet, your luscious thighs, your . . ."

"I get the picture!"

He stopped inside the bathroom door as Quinn pulled fresh towels from the linen closet. Taking them from her hands, he pulled her naked body close. A broad grin creased his lean face as he whispered, "Promise me something."

"What?" she asked suspiciously.

"Promise you'll be gentle with me."

Pulling from his grasp, Quinn winked lewdly. "Trust me."

"Sure. But will you respect me in the morning?" Tossing the towels on the counter, he pulled her into the shower.

"Now, let's see," he said, gently nuzzling behind her ear, "what was that you said about gentle?"

The warm water coursing over her skin, combined with Gabe's skillful ministrations, rekindled the last embers of her passion. His soap-slickened hands skimmed her body, igniting tiny bolts of electricity along their path. Stopping their exploration long enough to pull her to him, he lowered his head until his mouth captured hers. Gently teasing her lips.

He twisted his head until his luscious lips were level with her ear lobe. With soft, heated breath, his mouth sought the tender flesh of her lobe and nibbled gently.

Charged with sudden desire, Quinn raised her mouth and trailed kisses along the plane of his chin.

Gabe groaned and twisted until his back was against the tile walls, then he pulled her supple body against him.

She could feel the hardness of his thigh against her leg, his masculine strength the perfect counterpoint for the softness of her womanhood.

Then, cupping her face with his palms, he allowed his lips to explore with abandon. He started with her temple, where her wet tresses gently flowed like fall flowers, spilled from a flawless vase.

She quivered with delight as his lips moved, first to kiss each of her eyelids, then the tip of her nose. Teasing, he allowed his mouth to caress the corners of hers, then her chin.

She arched, demanding his kiss. Her mouth ached with reawakened longing. She was lost. All that existed was his musky scent, his provocative touch and the hot blood coursing wildly through her veins.

Finally, his mouth again captured hers. Testing. Savoring. Until at last he parted her lips and deepened his kiss. His hand slid down her shoulder, sending shockwaves into her stomach, searing the tender flesh.

Quinn was on fire. Coals that she had believed long dead, had only been banked. Beneath Gabe's expert touch, Quinn's passion now smoldered and leapt to life, glowing with a hot, white flame.

The water flowed over them, filling the small cubicle with a steam that echoed their steamy passion.

His wet, questing fingers moved up, finding and caressing the tender buds that crowned her breasts. She moaned with the exquisite torture, then arched her hips to meet the unquestionable proof that his passion equaled hers.

"Oh, Quinn," he murmured against her breast, "my sweet, sweet darling."

His hand moved down until it touched her sweet, moist center, causing a moan to erupt from her sensation-wracked lips.

Gabe slipped his palms beneath her firm buttocks and pulled her up, onto him.

Quinn gasped as she felt him inside her. Filling her. Her mind was a kaleidoscope of exploding color. Bursting sound. Her pounding heart threatened to leap out of her chest.

"Quinn, Quinn, darling. I . . . can't wait."

"Yes, yes, my sweet. Now. Oh, now." She pressed her face against his wet hair and drank in its sweetness. Gabe. Gabe. Gabe.

He was the beginning, the middle and the end of her universe.

Tears of joy ran down her face, mixing freely with the cooling shower as a fresh flow of lava erupted within her, sending forth its molten liquid through to her intimate places.

They held one another for a long, long time until at last the hot water gave out. Wordlessly, Gabe turned off the faucet and reached outside the stall for a towel. Wrapping it around her quivering body, he pulled her close and kissed the top of her head.

What they had found together was so priceless—so phenomenal—they were afraid to speak. Afraid the outside world would shatter the magic.

By the time Marla left, around noon, the rain had let up enough so that Gabe announced he thought the roads were passable.

The second phone call of their morning had come shortly after the lovers had left the shower.

Fortunately, Quinn mused, the phone call hadn't come a few moments earlier.

It had been one of Gabe's clients, frantic over some financial statement generated by a program on his computer that he didn't understand. He needed Gabe in the city. Right away.

So much for being rained in, she thought philosophically.

"I'll be back before dark, darling," Gabe said, tugging on his corduroy jacket. "And don't forget Marla's right across the street if you need anything."

Quinn smothered a grin. Marla had been right across the street for the past three years. Where before Quinn would have resented and felt smothered by a man's protectiveness, today she relished his concern.

"I'll be fine, trust me. Now give me a kiss and get going."

"You're sure?" His brows dipped in a frown. "I mean, this isn't *that* big a client. I could cancel."

"Don't be ridiculous. Now the sooner you get going the sooner you'll be back."

"Okay. You're right."

Gabe crossed the room in two long strides and knelt down beside her. Cupping her chin in his hand, he looked deeply into her velvet brown eyes. "About last night . . . and this morning, well, it was . . . I mean, we were . . . pretty special."

"I know."

He trailed his forefinger along her cheek. "God, your skin is so soft. Like your insides. You try so hard to be a tough cookie, but inside—inside you're all honey and marshmallow."

She blushed with pleasure. "I take it that's a compliment?"

Gabe ran a hand through his rumpled hair. "Now who can't be serious? I mean it, Quinn. The thing I love most about you is that I know who you are. You're the same on the inside as that wonderful soft skin on the outside. You're honest to a fault—your prices at the Scarecrow Emporium prove that! You know, when you operate in the kind of business arena that I do, you come across some pretty unscrupulous people from time to time."

Quinn wondered if that was an oblique reference to Tiffany, his ex-wife.

Gabe continued, "Believe me, babe. Trust and respect are the two most important ingredients in a relationship."

"Of course, a little lust helps," Quinn said in an attempt to lighten the mood somewhat. All of Gabe's talk about trust and honesty was starting to make her nervous.

"Amen to lust," he conceded. "But, still, when a man comes across a woman as honest and straightforward as you, well, he knows he'd better treasure you. And I do. Treasure you, I mean."

He kissed her then. Where their earlier kisses had been hard and almost wild with passion, today, this kiss, with its infinite sweetness, was like the sealing of a pact.

Then he was gone.

The empty house rattled around her. Despite having lived alone and been content with her own company for years, Quinn suddenly found no comfort in her solitude.

She missed Gabe.

He'd only been gone two hours, yet it seemed like days. She was becoming increasingly aware of how barren her life would be once he was gone for good.

Quinn was sitting in her usual spot by the front window when the mailman drove up. She watched him trudge up the steep stairs. He had quite a bundle in his fist. It would never all fit in her mailbox.

Oh, well, it was time for a little exercise anyway.

She heaved herself up and carefully braced the crutches under her arms. With a hesitant wobble befitting an inebriated penguin, she hobbled to the front door.

"Well, hi there, Ms. Rosetti. Long time, no see." Bob Waters, the mailman, was an expert in the collection and usage of cliches.

Quinn pointed to her bandaged ankle. "Been off my feet a while." Bob Waters wasn't the only person who could toss around trite phrases with abandon.

He helped her carry the bundle of mail into the living room then tipped his hat. "Gotta be going on my rounds. You take care now. Next time I see you, I want you to be putting your best foot forward, hear?"

"Loud and clear, Bob. Loud and clear." Not bad today, she thought. Matched him cliche for cliche.

When the door closed behind him, she picked up the mail. Utility bill. Advertisement. Coupons. Another bill. Then, on the bottom, a large manila envelope.

Quinn turned it over. The return address was Kresge, McGuire & Shaw, Attorneys at Law. With a feeling of dread, she tore open the envelope. Inside was a video cassette tape and a single sheet of typewritten paper:

MS. ROSETTI:

AS WE DISCUSSED IN MY OFFICE SEVERAL WEEKS AGO, WE ARE WINDING DOWN TO THE FINAL STAGES OF PROBATING MRS. FEATHERSTONE'S WILL. TO ACHIEVE THAT END, YOU WILL FIND ENCLOSED A VIDEO TAPE WHICH MRS. FEATHERSTONE MADE IN MY OFFICE WHEN SHE EXECUTED HER NEW WILL. IT WAS HER WISH THAT YOU AND MR. HUNTER VIEW THIS FILM TOGETHER BEFORE WE DISBURSE THE FUNDS.

MY SECRETARY WILL SCHEDULE A JOINT APPOINTMENT FOR YOU AND MR. HUNTER TO COME INTO MY OFFICE TO SIGN THE FINAL DOCUMENTS. A DRAFT FROM MY TRUST ACCOUNT WILL BE MADE AVAILABLE TO YOU AT THAT TIME.

THANK YOU FOR HELPING US WITH OUR INVESTIGATION OF MR. HUNTER. I AM SURE YOUR OBSERVATIONS OF HIM WILL BE AN INVALUABLE TOOL IN DETERMINING MRS. FEATHERSTONE'S HEIR.

VERY TRULY YOURS,

It was signed George Shaw.

Her heart flopped.

Well, the dreaded day was here. It had been simmering

in the back of her mind for days, weeks even. Quinn knew she had been secretly hoping that the whole thing would just go away.

How was she going to analyze Gabe's suitability impartially after all that had happened between them? Impossible.

Worse, she had somehow hoped that Gabe would never find out about her participation in his inheritance. What would he think when they were both called to Mr. Shaw's office? When Mr. Shaw announced that Quinn had been secretly evaluating him for the past several weeks?

And, worst of all, what would he think when Mr. Shaw handed her a check and thanked her for her help?

"Knock, knock, you home, Quinn?" Marla called from the foyer.

"In here." Quinn's voice was weak and thready.

One look at her friend's pale face and Marla dropped beside her on the sofa. Wrapping an arm around Quinn's trembling shoulder, she asked, "What is it, Quinnie? What's happened?"

"The end of the world."

In a few short breaths, Quinn explained that she had ignored Marla's advice and had never told Gabe about the appraisal she was supposed to submit to Attorney Shaw. And, now, they were supposed to meet jointly in Shaw's office for the dissemination of the estate's proceeds.

"Oh, Quinn! I told you this would happen. You knew he'd find out."

"Maybe if I tell him first, before he finds out from the lawyer! Do you think I could make him understand? After all, it isn't as if I've done anything really wrong."

But her conscience told her different. While her actions were not illegal, and possibly not even immoral—Quinn knew in her heart that she had been unethical. Once having undertaken the responsibility of giving a character evaluation of Gabriel Hunter, she should never have become involved with him.

Marla's noncommittal shrug told her the same thing.

"Oh, Quinn, I understand. I do. But once you became involved with him you should've called the lawyer and disqualified yourself."

"How could I do that? Mr. Shaw made it clear that if I backed out for any reason, Gabe will be completely disinherited."

Marla sighed. "And if you told him about what the old lady wanted you to do, then that would disqualify him, too, huh?"

Quinn nodded, her eyes moist with unshed tears of frustration. She just couldn't do that to him.

"Marla," she sniffed, "do you think Gabe will believe me? Why I agreed to do this, I mean?"

Looking off into space, Marla's mumbled response was not very comforting. "Sure, he'll believe you. I would."

Maybe, Quinn thought, Gabe would, too. For a while. But eventually he would wonder if her true motivation wasn't to qualify for her own bequest—the money that would give her five years' breathing room to build her own business. Five years to bring her father home.

He'd already had one gold-digging woman in his life. How could he not suspect her of being another?

Quinn thoughtfully scratched McLeish behind the ears. If their situations were reversed, she wondered, would she believe Gabe?

She shook her head doubtfully.

No. No matter what, she'd already lost Gabe. But she couldn't stand to see the disappointment in his eyes when he found out the truth. When he'd think she had used him for her own financial gain. She had to break off the relationship. Now. Before he found out the whole story from George Shaw.

There was no other way.

FOURTEEN

Quinn slung the handbag strap over her shoulder. She'd babied herself long enough—time to get back to work.

When Gabe came back that evening, she would tell him clearly and calmly that it was time for him to leave. For good. Let him think what he wanted, that she was bored with him or that she had another relationship. Whatever.

A week from now he'd be so glad to be back on his own turf that he'd hardly miss her.

In a month he'd be thankful.

In a year . . . in a year she doubted he'd even remember her name.

All Quinn knew was that she couldn't bear to see the disappointment and contempt in his golden eyes when he found out about her role in Elvira Featherstone's will. Her face flamed with self-disgust when she thought how naive and arrogant she had been—to deign to judge the worthiness of someone she had never met. And now the punishment of Daniel's whimsical Gods was being exacted. The price was Gabe's love.

She took a deep breath, steeling herself for the empty future.

It took her almost five minutes to traverse the short

distance between her front door and the Volkswagen parked in the drive. She wasn't quite used to the crutches yet and the soggy earth added an extra dimension of treachery. But she made it.

One thing about Quinn Rosetti, she thought, no matter how tough the challenge, she always made it.

She looked up and saw McLeish framed in the window, watching her with approval—Daniel Two was draped from his mouth.

"So what," she murmured, blinking back fresh tears, "it was just another monkey."

Feeling pretty righteous about conquering the stairs, she pushed the crutches over to the passenger side of the car and inserted the key. She released the handbrake and put the gear into reverse. Holding her breath, Quinn took her right foot off the brake.

So far so good, she thought as the little Bug slowly rolled down the steep driveway and into the street.

"Oh!" She gasped with pain when she pressed too hard engaging the clutch with her injured foot. After resting a moment, she tried again. Slower this time.

Okay, she thought, a little twinge, but not bad.

Soon she had the hang of this new driving technique and the little car sputtered into town.

Idyllwild's picturesque downtown area could have been lifted from the front of a postcard. Everything was new-penny bright from the rain. In the distance, Lily Rock, the monolith that stood watch over the small community, glistened in the morning light.

Like Gabe once stood watch over her. She bit her lip at the memory of his gentle protectiveness. *Stop it. Stop torturing yourself,* she admonished.

Forcing herself to concentrate on the quaint beauty of the village, Quinn drove slowly, soaking up the atmosphere. Like a Currier & Ives lithograph, the Alpine-styled shops were donned in their holiday finery. White lights twinkled from bare tree limbs. Chimneys boasted clouds of fragrant woodsmoke while crystal dewdrops sparkled from every surface.

She felt herself being revived. Resuscitated by the crisp, clean air, redolent of cedar and pine. She couldn't imagine anyone giving up this mountain freshness for city smog. But Gabe would.

With a snarl of self-rebuke, she forced Gabe into a dark closet in the back of her mind. Now, if he'd just stay there.

Parking the car in the city lot in the center of town, Quinn floundered across the street. Between the shifting gravel surface and the unwieldy crutches, she almost fell twice, but soon gained her footing and completed the short walk.

Fumbling in her purse for the spare key to the Scarecrow Emporium, Quinn stopped dead in her tracks.

The front window display was an adorable scene of Santa's workshop, complete with elves, Santa and even a twig reindeer with a red nose. Mrs. Claus was standing beside a kitchen table, covered with a red-checked cloth, putting the finishing touches on a pie so realistic Quinn could almost smell it.

It was cute. It was eye-catching. It wasn't hers.

"Damn you to hell, Gabriel Hunter!" She pushed her key in the lock and slammed the door open.

She'd *thought* they'd had an understanding. She explicitly told him she didn't want to change the window display until after Thanksgiving. That was still a week away, the display she had left in the window had incorporated both Halloween and Thanksgiving.

Gabe had intentionally countermanded her instructions. Mr. Marketing Genius knew best.

What other changes had he instituted behind her back?

She stormed about the small boutique, taking inventory and comparing prices. Everything was different. Every item in stock boasted a new price tag. Each price had been raised fifteen, and in some cases twenty, percent.

Not content, he had continued to undermine her by shifting displays and adding a small cabinet to hold the miniature scarecrows.

Quinn stood in the middle of the store that no longer seemed hers and blinked back tears. She didn't know what hurt the worst, his deceit or the fact that the changes were good. Excellent in fact.

Stalking into the stockroom, Quinn looked for her account book. Again, she hardly recognized the place. Neat. Tidy. Everything in a specific place. Floor swept clean of debris. In a few short weeks, Gabriel Hunter had managed to implement all of the changes she had been planning for three years and never found the time.

A sharp nudge in her ego reminded her that he had made a few valuable changes she had never imagined.

Quinn flipped open the ledger. At least he hadn't changed her bookkeeping system. Not yet anyway. Probably a good thing she'd come back early.

Sitting down at her scarred wooden desk, she ran a finger over the totals for the previous Saturday. There was some mistake! The Emporium had never had a *week* this lucrative, much less a single day.

Quinn slammed the book closed. Everything checked out. Gross profits had increased tenfold. Why didn't that make her feel better?

Instead it made the pain sharper. Fed her anger. Fueled her bruised ego. What made him think he had the right to make these changes? And, worse, why had he succeeded so spectacularly when her profits were barely adequate?

And why did she feel lessened by his successes?

Leaning back in the rickety chair, she examined her own motivations. Was it simply pride that made her resist all of Gabe's suggestions? She hoped not. But she couldn't think of another reason.

Was she really so insecure of her own talents that she would deliberately turn down valuable help? She was a better person than that. Wasn't she?

Deep inside Quinn knew that some small, selfish part of her was jealous. Envious of Gabe's success at *her* business. Resentful that he hadn't wanted or needed her help. And bitter because he was no longer a part of her life. They couldn't share this success—or anything else any longer.

But this new, unsettling glimpse of the truth didn't help Quinn let go of her anger. Instead, she nursed it like a child with its bedtime bottle. Sipping slowly on her injured pride and fondling her broken heart, she turned her disappointment into resentment of Gabe.

He probably thought he was doing her a big favor. Maybe he considered this repayment for services rendered? Well, this was still her business and Mr. Gabriel Hunter was going to learn a thing or two about butting into other people's businesses.

When Gabe opened the front door that evening, Quinn was waiting by the fireplace.

"Hi, babe!" He carried a large, bulky package wrapped with brown paper. His face was alive with an expectant smile. Midway across the room, he stopped, his smile fading. "What's wrong?"

Quinn held her hand out, palm up. "Perhaps," she said in an icy voice, "you'd be so kind as to return my keys. To my shop as well as my home."

Gabe's brow furrowed. He dropped the package on the floor and grasped her shoulders with his strong hands. "What's happened?"

"Nothing that need concern you. Please just give me my keys."

He tightened his grip until her face paled. He dropped his hands to his sides, like they were glowing coals. "Don't play games, just tell me why you're upset."

"Upset? I am hurt, bitter, enraged, furious, incensed, and teed-off. Upset is a little mild for what I'm feeling right now."

He reached in his pocket and withdrew a key ring. With slow deliberation he dislodged two keys and dropped them onto the coffee table. "I can see that. Mind telling me what great sin I seem to have committed?"

"I was at the Emporium today, Gabe! I saw all the changes you made."

"I can explain . . ."

"I have eyes, you don't need to explain. You deliberately disregarded my instructions and changed my store to suit your ideas. You played shopkeeper with my money. You speculated with my future! How could you, Gabe?"'

His jaw clenched tightly, he stalked from the room and returned with a manila folder. He threw it on the coffee table beside the keys. "My *speculations* netted you a forty-three percent profit gain in a little over two weeks."

"But what if you'd lost money? I'm not a big corporation. I can't afford to take chances."

"Wow, I'm overwhelmed by your faith in my abilities, Quinn. Do you really think that I'd have made changes without a solid basis for my decisions?"

"You should have discussed it with me first!"

"I tried, remember? Quinn, I have fourteen years' experience salvaging small businesses. One look at your books told me you were in serious financial trouble. But you didn't want to face that. You wanted to keep your head buried like a damned ostrich and hope everything would just go away!"

"But you had no right . . ."

"I had every right! I love you and, stupid me, I thought you loved me, too."

When she said nothing, he pressed his advantage. "Everything I have is yours, you know that. That's what love's all about, Quinn. Sharing. Trusting."

"That's not fair. Love has nothing to do with this."

"Apparently not." He ran splayed fingers through his hair. "I thought I was doing you a favor. It seemed to me that you were more interested in the creative side of your business and didn't have a lot of fascination with the marketing side. So I thought—hey, we complement each other. I'll help her with the finances and she can create to her heart's content. What did you think, Quinn, that I was going to cheat you?"

She turned away, and swiped at the tears that were flowing down her cheeks. He was right. About everything. It had only been her foolish pride that had kept her from listening to him in the first place. Knowing what was coming, maybe she engineered this whole thing so she'd have a valid reason to break off their relationship when things got too complicated.

Gabe stood still, waiting for her to speak. He looked confused. Bewildered. As if he couldn't understand how their relationship had gotten so out of kilter in a matter of a few hours.

More than anything in the world, Quinn wanted to throw herself in his arms and apologize. She knew Gabe wouldn't even demand the apology. She could read it in his eyes that he just wanted them to talk.

But she couldn't.

"Quinn? Tell me what's really going on. What's really bothering you?"

Tell him what was really going on? How could she tell him the truth about Elvira's will? Knowing her financial situation as intimately as he did, would he have any doubt that her only interest was in the inheritance?

He'd been burned once, and badly, by a woman motivated by greed. She'd rather die than have him think she, too, cared more about money than love.

Wiping away the last vestiges of her tears, she turned back to face him. "Nothing. We have nothing further to talk about."

"You're sure, then?"

She nodded. Weak at first, then stronger. "Yes," she lied, "I'm sure."

"I see." He picked up the package that he'd discarded

on the floor. "Here, I brought you a present." The package hit the carpet with a soft whoosh as he dropped it at her feet.

Without another word, Gabe walked quietly from the room, leaving Quinn with her broken heart.

He returned a few minutes later, his suitcase in hand. "I thought we were good together, Quinn," he said quietly, his amber eyes dark with pain. "I don't understand why you want to throw it all away."

He turned to go and stepped on a piece of paper that had fallen from the coffee table. He bent over to pick it up, then stopped.

The suitcase slid unnoticed from his grip. He pivoted on one heel to face her. Waving the single sheet of bond paper in front of him, he demanded, "What's this all about, Quinn? This letter from George Shaw."

Oh, lord, it was all for nothing. With a faltering voice she tried to explain how Elvira's will had roped her into doing an assessment of his character.

Gabe dropped the paper like it was aflame. "Wait a minute, let me understand this. The whole time I've been here, you've been watching my every move with the intention of writing a report on my character? And you had the nerve to accuse me of doing something underhanded behind your back?"

"I know it looks like that, but it's not exactly . . ."

"Then exactly like how, Quinn? And this bequest to you—pretty substantial I would suppose?"

She covered her face with her hands, not wanting to face the contempt mirrored in his eyes. "I don't know the exact amount, but it would pay for my father's nursing and my living expenses for five years so I could develop the Scarecrow Emporium. Maybe start a franchise."

"Ah. I see. Well, no wonder you weren't concerned about the financial health of your business. You didn't need my help—you'd already covered all your bets."

"That's not true! One thing has nothing to do with the other."

"Doesn't it?" he asked. His mouth curled up in open contempt. "*Money's never been important to me.* Sound familiar? How about, *I've never cared much about possessions.* Remember saying those things to me, Quinn? Lies. All lies."

Gabe picked his suitcase back up. His voice was cold, calm. Deadly calm and dripping with disgust. "Then, to cover your own deceit, you pick some ridiculous fight and blame me? God, what a fool I've been. I really believed you, Quinn. I really loved you."

Quinn turned her head from the betrayal and disappointment that crushed his shoulders in defeat.

She had no defense.

When she looked up, he was walking away. Out the door and out of her life.

Forever.

FIFTEEN

"Gabe, wait!"

He turned from the doorway. "Why, do you want to tell me some more lies? How about last night, Quinn? This morning. Were you evaluating me then, too? Tell me, *love*," the word slithered from his lips like a deadly viper, "on a scale of one to ten, how did I score?"

His words were a physical blow, knocking her speechless. Sticks and stones could never be as hurtful as the words hovering in the air between them.

Quinn lowered her gaze beneath his blistering wrath. When she looked up, he was gone.

A moment later, she heard the front door latch quietly behind him.

She watched from the window as he waded through the marshy yard. Watched her life walk away.

Suddenly, she realized the phone was ringing. Without thought, like a zombie on the late movie, she reached over and picked up the receiver.

"Hello?"

"Quinn? Dr. Johnson here."

"Oh, hello, doctor. Is anything wrong?"

He chuckled across the line. "No, not a thing. But

listen, the wife and I are heading out of town this weekend for a little R & R in Hawaii. So, I'm calling all my patients to give them Dr. Chesterton's phone number as a back-up. Got a pencil?"

"Uh. Just a moment." She fumbled in the drawer of the end table until she found a stub and an old crumpled envelope. She couldn't believe she was moving. Functioning. How could she still be talking when her soul was dead? "Go ahead, doctor."

He gave her the back-up physician's number then asked, "By the way, is that Hunter fellow still in town? I thought I'd better give him the number, too."

"Why?"

"Well, I know he just sprained his wrist that day, but what with carrying you around I've been a little concerned about the way it's healing. It's still bothering him considerably, you know."

Quinn shook her head. "Dr. Johnson, I'm confused. What sprained wrist?"

There was silence on the line for a moment. Then he said, "Well, I don't know. I mean if he didn't tell you about it, then maybe I shouldn't . . ."

"You've already told me. He's just being a martyr. How can I help him take care of it if I don't know about the injury?"

The doctor thought for a moment. "I guess that's true. After all, you did come into the office together."

Quinn listened in shock as Dr. Johnson related the story. Bits and pieces came from her own memory, like lost pieces of a jigsaw puzzle. The way he'd known Dr. Johnson's name before she told him. The white bandage she'd mistaken for thermal underclothing. So many other signs. So obvious, if she'd been looking for them. If she hadn't been so involved in her own woes.

Apparently it had happened the same day that McLeish ran amuck. Somehow he had sprained his wrist chasing the cat after he slid in the spilled paint. Gabe had found Dr.

Johnson's name in her address book and gone for treatment. He had just returned when he found her sobbing on the bedroom floor.

In a flash of clarity, Quinn remembered his pale face. Of course, he had been in pain—not angry as she'd supposed. That flash of white she'd seen beneath his shirtsleeve; not long underwear, but a bandage wrap for his wrist.

So many clues but she'd been too blind, too self-asorbed to see them.

Nor had Gabe mentioned his injury. Not even when he had carried her to the car, and lifted her frequently for those first few days. How that must have hurt!

Quinn thanked the doctor and replaced the receiver.

She looked out the window. To her surprise, Gabe was still wrestling to fit his suitcase into the back seat of his sports car. Marla was standing next to him, her arms gesturing wildly. Gabe was jabbing the suitcase with all his strength, missing the door opening. Quinn smiled in gentle amusement, watching his efforts. Sometimes he's such a klutz, she thought fondly.

But sometimes he was really wonderful, she reminded herself. Not once did he mention his own pain while he waited on her hand and foot.

What a fool she'd been. That man was her hero! Why hadn't she just told him the truth and hang the consequences? Marla said the peculiar provisions of Elvira's will probably wouldn't hold up in court. But she hadn't trusted Marla's judgment either.

No, Ms. Independence had to chart her own course and follow it blindly. No matter the cost.

If she'd just had faith in Gabe. He would have understood she wasn't after his money. Would she think that of him if the tables were turned? Of course not.

Quinn jumped at the sound of the front door opening. She whirled around. Gabe's tall, lean frame was silhouetted in the open archway. *He'd come back!*

"I forgot the cat," he muttered, his voice as frigid as the Arctic winds in January.

Whatever the reason, now that she had him, he wasn't going to get away again. Not until she'd done her best to make him understand.

He stalked into the hall and returned a moment later with the white plastic cat carrier. "Where is he? Never mind, I'll find him myself."

His long, angry strides carried him toward the bedrooms.

She had to talk to him, make him understand. But how? Anger and betrayal had captured his reason. He wouldn't listen to anything she had to say.

Somehow, someway she had to make him stay long enough to hear her out. She couldn't physically detain him . . . unless . . .

No, that was crazy! She couldn't hold him prisoner.

He was in the guest bedroom, calling the cat. She had to act. Now. As soon as he corralled McLeish, he'd be out that door again.

Fate had given her a second chance, she wasn't going to let it go by.

Heedless of her now-throbbing ankle, Quinn hobbled to the front door. Frantically, she locked the door and dropped the key into her pocket.

She heard Gabe's footsteps. He'd left the guest room and was headed for the workshop. She had to hurry!

With uneven, faltering steps Quinn rushed to the kitchen. Gabe was coming—his steps echoed right behind her. No sooner had she finished locking the back door, and pulled the key from the old-fashioned lock when Gabe's shadow fell over her.

"What the hell do you think you're doing?"

Slowly, she turned around and leaned against the door. Her foot was pulsating with the strain. Tears of love and desperation slid freely down her face. What if he truly no longer wanted her? She'd be making a fool of herself for nothing.

Suddenly that didn't matter. Her dignity was of little value without Gabe.

"You're not leaving here until you listen to me," she said, wiping a trail of dampness from her cheek.

Gabe's golden eyes flashed dangerously. "Surely it's not your intention to take me prisoner? That's a little bizarre, even for you."

"You can make fun all you want, Gabe Hunter. But you're going to give me the chance to explain. You owe me that much."

"I owe you nothing."

"Maybe not, but . . ." this was it, she thought, her last trump card. "If you don't give me ten minutes, you'll never see one penny of your inheritance. I'll write a report that will singe the hair off of George Shaw's toupee."

Gabe's harsh laugh split the air. "Charming, Quinn. First kidnapping and now blackmail. What's your ace in the hole—murder?"

She raised her chin and looked him square in the eyes but said nothing. This was her whole life she was gambling with. Nothing would make her back down now.

"All right, Quinn. I'll play out this hand. But shall we go into the living room where we can be more comfortable?"

She limped back into the living room and sank gratefully onto the sofa.

Gabe perched on the edge of the easy chair, like he might bolt at any provocation. "Okay, Quinn. I believe it's your lead."

Drawing a deep breath, trying to inhale every ounce of courage, she began. "It started last spring when I found this little kitten . . ."

Gabe looked at his watch and stood up. "That was an amusing little story, but I believe your ten minutes are up now."

The pain in Quinn's heart throbbed anew. He still didn't believe her! And why should he, she thought glumly. She could hardly believe herself as she recounted that fantastic story.

Of course, in time, she could prove it to him. George Shaw could verify the facts. Marla. But somehow she knew in her heart that if Gabe walked out that door that they'd never recover what they'd lost.

But how could she make him understand?

The only other thing she could think of was the video cassette tape from the attorney's office. There might be something in that tape that would cut through Gabe's hurt and anger. But she hadn't seen the tape. What if it only made matters worse?

Gabe's toe tapped the carpeted floor in impatience. "Are you going to unlock the door or do I bust it down?"

Think, Quinn. Do something. Anything.

Suddenly, she remembered when Gabe had picked up and carried that disgusting field mouse. He hadn't wanted to do that. But at that time he'd drawn his courage from her need. She could do no less than to follow his example.

She picked the cartridge up from the coffee table.

"You read George Shaw's letter," she said to his questioning look, "Elvira wanted us to watch this together."

Gabe shook his head. "I don't want to see it. You can tell Shaw to give my share to the Home for Wayward Cats. I'm through."

"Gabe, please." Her voice broke. "If you want me to beg?"

A shadow, dark like her pain, flashed through his eyes. "No," he said finally. "I don't want you to beg. I'll watch it."

Taking the cassette from her hand he inserted it into the VCR.

The screen quivered and jerked then filled with Elvira Featherstone's genial face. She was sitting in the leather wing chair in George Shaw's office. McLeish was ensconced in her lap.

Is this damned thing on, George? Oh, it is. So I just go ahead? All right.

Hello, Gabriel. Quinn. I hope you don't mind my coming back to haunt you like this, but I didn't know any other way to do this.

I'm afraid I've played a pretty dirty trick on you both. But it's your own fault, you know. She waggled a bony finger at the camera. *I tried to get the two of you together for months but both of you were too afraid to take the chance. Imagine, being so conventional at your ages! Chance is what life's all about.*

Anyway, by now I suppose the jig is up, you found me out. But wasn't it worth the effort? I can see the two of you right now, side-by-side, watching this together. You're thinking, the old broad knew what she was doing, aren't you, Gabriel?

Elvira turned away from the camera to put McLeish on the floor. Now, where was I? Oh, yes. My inheritance. Well, obviously this whole thing has been an elaborate ploy to get the two of you together. I just knew if I could get you two to spend some time with one another that you'd fall in love—just as I love you both. I was right wasn't I, Quinn? Of course, I was.

From the corner of her eye, Quinn stole a look at Gabe. His expression inscrutable, he was nevertheless enraptured by the scene playing on the television screen.

And that evaluation thing, Elvira continued. *Silly, wasn't it? George told me it would never work, that Quinn would never fall for it. But, pardon me, dear, but you're such an innocent I never had a doubt you'd agree to do it. And do an admirable job. By the way, what is your opinion of Gabriel?*

Now, Quinn could feel Gabe's eyes on her. She didn't dare look up. Would she see forgiveness or contempt?

Of course, my little scheme would never have worked if Quinn had known me better. That's why I endeavored to keep our friendship confined to telephone conversations.

Imagine, Gabriel, anyone believing I needed help deciding whether or not I liked someone? As if I ever needed assistance forming an opinion.

Now, Quinn did look up. The tightness had eased from Gabe's face and he was nodding his head, agreeing with his great-aunt's statements.

Well, that's about it, my darlings. Quinn, I have, of course, made provisions for a trust fund on your behalf, as promised. Gabriel, after a few small bequests, my estate is yours. Do with it what you will. I would like you both to take care of McLeish during his lifetime. It's my hope, of course, that you'll be together anyway.

At the older woman's impatient gesture, the camera moved in for a close-up. *The main thing I'd like to leave you both is love. Embrace life. Embrace each other. Take chances. You've both had hard knocks in romance, but who hasn't? Those awful experiences help you appreciate the right person when you find them. It's my fervent hope that, in each other, you've found the right persons.*

Ciao, my darlings. Have a good life. She winked, a broad, almost lewd wink from an eighty-year old woman who still knew how to enjoy life to the very end. *Ta-ta.*

The scene wobbled and in the background they could hear Elvira shouting at George Shaw to turn the damned thing off.

With a deep sigh, Gabe stood up and flicked off the television. For long moments he stood with his back to Quinn. Unreadable. Unapproachable.

Finally, he turned. "Quinn, I . . ."

"Oh, Gabe . . ." True to form, their tortured voices rang out at the same moment.

He held up his hand. "No, Quinn. This time I go first." When she didn't argue, he continued. "I've been a blind, egocentric, insensitive, oafish jerk. And those are my good points."

"Oh, Gabe, that's not . . ."

He held up a hand. "No, wait. Let me finish. If you're

willing to have me, although the good Lord alone knows why you'd want to, I want you for my wife. But that's only if you're willing to make a lifetime commitment."

Quinn sprang up from the sofa. In her excitement, she'd put too much pressure on her sore foot.

"Oof!" She gasped and started to fall.

But Gabe's quick responses helped him to catch her at the last second. Scooping her into his strong arms, he cuddled her to the warm wall of his chest.

"My darling, darling Quinn. What did we almost do?" he murmured, lips brushing her hair.

He carried her to the sofa and lowered her gently, like a priceless treasure, to the soft cushions.

Quinn clung tightly to his neck, trailing tear-dampened kisses all over his face.

He smiled, that wonderful, crooked . . . sexy . . . grin that filled the dreariest room with sunshine. She placed her palms on both sides of his face, delighting in the slight scratchiness of his five o'clock shadow. Oh, how her heart thrilled at the sight of him. The feel of him. The luscious taste of him.

She couldn't get enough. She didn't want to let him go. Ever.

Suddenly, a wicked smile played across her wide, sensuous mouth. She didn't *have* to let him go. Gabriel Hunter—gentle, playful, thoughtful, impetuous—was hers, in all of his complexity. As she was his.

She wanted to run outdoors and shout at the world—GABE HUNTER LOVES ME! But she couldn't release the hold on his neck long enough to go anywhere.

For the first time in her life she felt free. Free in her love. To touch and explore without reservation. Free to laugh and cry, knowing she was safe in the haven of his love.

Wrapping her long legs around his waist, she pulled him on top of her. Her fingers traced the strong planes of his face, embedding the feel in her memory for all time. Then her hands slid down the column of his neck, smoothing along the width of his shoulders. Fingers alive with the feel of him, she allowed her hands to explore his chest. His taut abdomen.

"Quinn, darling, what are you trying to do to me?" Gabe groaned against her neck.

"Everything, my love," she murmured, "everything."

"Mmmm. I'm marrying a wanton temptress."

Quinn's agile fingers found the buckle of his trousers. "Wait until I show you how wanton," she breathed.

Gabe leaned back, rejoicing in the love she was unashamedly showing him. At last, he reflected, she finally trusted him. He lay still, glorying in the touch of the woman he loved, until he could stand no more.

Twisting around in the confined space of the sofa, he pulled his beloved closer. Sliding his hand through the tumbled mass of her thick, auburn tresses, he pulled her face to his with a tortured moan.

Quinn's ecstatic sigh filled the air as his mouth found hers. Gabe gathered her in his arms, his kisses deepening in intensity until her breath came in short, shallow puffs. Tongues thrusting and joining. Seducing. Seeking.

The room spun and whirled, as she was giddily bewitched by the sweetness of his lips. She slid her arms up his back, crushing his chest against her breasts. Her nipples, hardened with arousal, were sensitive buds, blossoming at his touch.

"Oh, Gabe," her whisper was like the soft fluttering of butterfly wings in the quiet. "I need you. Please . . . my darling, now."

"Oh, yes, my sweet. Yes."

His hands, working their own sweet magic, freed them from their restraining clothing and she felt her hot flesh touch his. Gabe's hand trailed lightly from her breasts, across her stomach, gently gliding down her sleek thighs until he found the ready font of her femininity.

Pulling her beneath him, he entered her in one smooth

stroke. Their fire was too hot, too intense to burn long. Quinn arched to meet him, matching him thrust for thrust as his hardness cleaved deep inside her.

Then, like the molton flow of an erupting volcano, she felt the surge of her passion. Growing. Burbling. Filling her with a delicious heat that threatened to consume her. As Gabe's pace quickened, she arched her hips, grinding against him until they met at their peak.

Quinn sank back onto the cushions, pulling Gabe with her. They lay for long moments, breathing harshly, savoring the sweet afterglow of their love.

A few moments later, Gabe lifted his head and kissed her tenderly on the forehead. She looked into his dear eyes and saw her own love reflected in their golden depths.

Then, suddenly, Gabe pulled away.

She covered herself with the crocheted afghan from the back of the sofa and sat up, mystified. "Where are you going?"

"Just stay there. I forgot something." He stepped into his shorts. Wordlessly, he crossed the room and retrieved the bulky package he'd brought in earlier. He dropped it on the sofa beside her. Grinning like a small boy with a new puppy, he said, "Well, go on. Aren't you going to open it?"

Puzzled, Quinn reached for the parcel. It was surprisingly soft. Almost downy. She tore open the layers of brown wrapping paper.

Her fingers touched an exquisite silkiness.

Could it be? Hope bubbled like a wellspring in her chest. Ripping off the remaining paper, Quinn clutched the contents to her breast, and squealed, "My gramma's quilt! Oh, Gabe, how did you ever get all the paint off? It looks wonderful."

A gentle smile playing across his face, he touched the sweet smoothness of her cheek. "A friend of mine in L.A.—Madelyne Parker, you may have heard of her?

Anyway, she knew somebody in the dry cleaning game who she said was a miracle worker. Guess she was right.''

"Madelyne Parker?'' she gulped. "You mean blonde, gorgeous, sexy Madelyne Parker?''

Gabe chuckled. "Well, that's what Marty says, anyway.'' He cocked his head and gave her a smile bursting with mischief. "I did tell you the Parkers got back together, didn't I? Maybe I forgot. Anyway, they invited us up for a weekend.''

"Oh?''

"Yeah. I told them it wouldn't be for a while yet.''

Quinn narrowed her eyes in suspicion. "Why not?''

"Told them we were going to be on our honeymoon. An extended honeymoon.''

Quinn threw her arms around his neck, smothering him with wet, happy kisses.

Elvira Featherstone had indeed left her a fortune. And she was going to spend him wisely.

No. 34 NO EASY TASK by Chloe Summers
Hunter is wary when Doone delivers a package that will change his life.

No. 35 DIAMOND ON ICE by Lacey Dancer
Diana could melt even the coldest of hearts. Jason hasn't a chance.

No. 36 DADDY'S GIRL by Janice Kaiser
Slade wants more than Andrea is willing to give. Who wins?

No. 37 ROSES by Caitlin Randall
K.C. and Brett join forces to find who is stealing Brett's designs. But who will help them both when they find their hearts are stolen too?

No. 38 HEARTS COLLIDE by Ann Patrick
Matthew knew he was in trouble when he crashed into Paula's car but he never dreamed it would be this much trouble!

No. 39 QUINN'S INHERITANCE by Judi Lind
Quinn and Gabe find they are to share in a fortune. What they find is that they share much, much more—and it's priceless!

No. 40 CATCH A RISING STAR by Laura Phillips
Fame and fortune are great but Justin finds they are not enough. Beth, a red-haired, green-eyed bundle of independence is his greatest treasure.